William Bramley-Moore

The Six Sisters of the Valleys

An Historical Romance: Vol. I.

William Bramley-Moore

The Six Sisters of the Valleys
An Historical Romance: Vol. I.

ISBN/EAN: 9783337021009

Printed in Europe, USA, Canada, Australia, Japan

Cover: Foto ©Andreas Hilbeck / pixelio.de

More available books at **www.hansebooks.com**

THE

SIX SISTERS OF THE VALLEYS.

An Historical Romance.

BY THE

REV. WILLIAM BRAMLEY-MOORE, M.A.,

INCUMBENT OF GEBRARD'S CROSS, BUCKS.

WITH ILLUSTRATIONS DRAWN BY T. H. NICHOLSON, ENGRAVED
BY C. W. SHEERES.

"I declare that I feel an invincible horror for all tortures and violence
inflicted upon humanity under the pretext of serving or defending religion."
MONTALEMBERT, *August*, 1863.

IN THREE VOLUMES.

VOL. I.

LONDON:

LONGMAN, GREEN, LONGMAN, ROBERTS, AND GREEN.

1864.

MARBILD, PRINTER, LONDON.

TO THE MEMBERS

OF

THE WALDENSIAN CHURCH,

IN THE VALLEYS OF PIEDMONT,

THIS WORK,

ILLUSTRATING A PORTION OF THEIR FATHERS' HISTORY, AND
WHOSE SCENES ARE PRINCIPALLY LAID IN THE
VALLEY OF LUCERNA,

IS DEDICATED,

WITH FEELINGS OF ADMIRATION AND CHRISTIAN FELLOWSHIP,

BY THEIR OBEDIENT SERVANT,

THE AUTHOR.

PREFACE.

———◆———

THE following romance adheres, for the most part, rigidly to history, and presents a general sketch of the period in which the scene is laid. Almost every incident is based upon authentic facts, and the allusions in the conversations are more or less historical, and can be verified by references. If any details appear horrible, let truth be their apology. Yet let the reader remember that the half is not told. Nothing could exceed the cruelties and horrors that were actually perpetrated by the Roman Catholics against the Waldenses; the imagination can hardly conceive them, morality forbids us to blacken our pages with their exhumation, and they would be difficult to credit, were it not for the well-known evil of human nature, especially when excited by religious hatred and persecuting intolerance.

The writer is aware that in this present age of indifferentism he must submit to the charge of bigotry. Had the deeds mentioned in these volumes happened but once the accusation might be justified, but from their lamentable recurrence they cannot be looked upon as accidental outbursts; they have happened in every clime where the Roman Catholic religion is dominant, and must be considered as an intrinsic part of the genius of that system.

To prove that the events we relate have had their unhappy parallel in history, we may quote Hume's account of the massacre of the English Protestants in Ireland by the Papists in 1641 :—

" But death was the lightest punishment inflicted by those rebels. All the tortures which wanton cruelty could devise, all the lingering pains of body, the anguish of mind, the agonies of despair, could not satiate revenge excited without injury, and cruelty derived from no cause. To enter into particulars would shock the least delicate humanity. Such enormities, though attested by undoubted evidence, appear almost incredible. Depraved nature, even per-verted religion, encouraged by the utmost licence, reaches not to such a pitch of ferocity, unless the pity inherent in human breasts be destroyed by that con-tagion of example which transports men beyond all the usual motives of conduct and behaviour.

"Amidst all these enormities the sacred name of religion resounded on every side, not to stop the hands of these murderers, but to enforce their blows, and to steel their hearts against every movement of human or social sympathy. The English, as heretics, abhorred of God, and detestable to all holy men, were marked out by the priests for slaughter, and, of all actions, to rid the world of these declared enemies to Catholic faith and piety, was represented as the most meritorious. Nature, which in that rude people was sufficiently inclined to atrocious deeds, was farther stimulated by precept, and national prejudices empoisoned by those aversions, more deadly and incurable, which arose from an enraged superstition. While death finished the sufferings of each victim, the bigoted assassins, with joy and exultation, still echoed in his expiring ears, that these agonies were but the commencement of torments infinite and eternal."—Hume's *History of England*, vol. vi., chap. lv., p. 384.

Passages like these may rescue anything in the following pages from being deemed an exaggeration; but the well-nigh incredible cruelties of 1655 are well authenticated. Léger, the moderator of the Waldensian churches, and Sir Samuel Morland, the " commissioner extraordinary," sent by Cromwell, immediately after the massacres, to remonstrate with

the court of Turin, have left us the notarial deposi-
tions of the murderous incidents.   Europe was
thrilled with horror, Louis the XIVth (the future
revoker of the Edict of Nantes, 1685) wrote to the
Duke of Savoy, and as Englishmen we may feel proud
of the honourable part taken by this country, both
in protesting and in relieving the distressed.

Sir Samuel Morland wrote a history, entitled,
"The History of the Evangelical Church of the
Valleys of Piemont," to which reference may be
made at the British Museum, or at the Cambridge
University Library.   The following is his heading to
Book ii., Chapter vi., in which he gives the details
of the massacres :—

"A brief and most authentick narrative of some
part of those extraordinary cruelties which were
exercised against the poor Protestants in the Valleys
of Piemont during the heat of the late massacre, in
the year of our Lord 1655, in the month of April.
Every particular circumstance whereof was abun-
dantly verified to the authour, during his abode in
these parts, both by word of mouth, and by the
formal Attestations and Subscriptions of those very
persons who were both Eye and Ear witnesses of those
inhumane Cruelties, the true originals of some whereof he hath exposed to publick view in the Library of
the University of Cambridg, and for several weighty

Reasons hath reserved the rest in his own custody, ready to give any ingenuous person full and clear satisfaction."

His own speech before the Court of Turin, the attestation of the officer Du Petit Bourg, the remonstrances of the various courts of Europe, place the truth of these incidents beyond cavil.

Morland collected many original documents and manuscripts, and deposited them at Cambridge, where they now exist, to wit, the Bull of Innocent the VIIIth., Du Petit Bourg's attestation, The Factum of the Court of Turin, The Noble Leçon, and many others. These MSS. form twenty-one volumes, lettered from A to W. For many years the volumes from A to G were wanting, and it was supposed that they had been stolen in the reign of James II.

Dr. Gilly, in his " Waldensian Researches, 1831," page 157, discusses the question, and regrets the hopeless loss of these venerable documents. He says, page 156 :—

" Since the lost manuscripts were missing from the library in 1794 and in 1753, and no light was thrown at either of these periods upon the manner in which they had been removed, I fear all trace must now be considered as entirely gone, and nothing but accident will clear up the mystery which hangs about them."

des Champs, les autres au soin des Prairies, et a celuy des troupeaux de Vaches, de Brebis, ou de Chèvres. L'aîné des Frères, et sa Femme qui estoit l'aînée des Sœurs, estans le Père et la Mère de toute la Famille."—*Léger*, Part ii., chapter ix., page 122.

The following is Dr. Muston's translation, vol. i. page 352 :—

"'I cannot refrain from remarking here,' adds the historian, 'that there were six brothers of these Prinses, and that they had married six sisters, and all of them had numbers of children, and that they lived together without having ever made any division of their property, and without the slightest discord having ever been observed in that family. It was composed of more than forty persons, each of whom had his own department of labour ; some in the work of the vineyards and cultivation of the fields, others in the care of the meadows or in that of the flocks. The eldest of the brothers and his wife, who was also the eldest of the sisters, were like the father and mother of the whole family.' Yet these patriarchal scenes, so worthy of respect, so beautiful, so simple, and so Christian, furnished prey to the demon of Popery, trained to cruelty by superstition, and descending beneath the level of the savage."

When visiting the valleys in 1857, the author had the good fortune to procure an ancient copy of

"Léger's History," the very book, he believes, from which Rodolphe Peyran argued with Dr. Gilly, as mentioned by him, page 79, in his "Narrative of an Excursion to the Mountains of Piedmont in the Year 1823." This book suggested the following romance, and has been useful in its composition.

The liberties taken with the persons and places are slight. The Farm of La Baudène, which was near Villar, has been located nearer the entrance of the Valley of Lucerna, for the embodiment of Gastaldo's edict. The Valley of Lucerna is the same as that of the Val Pelice, although the latter has within the last three years become its official name. Joshua Janavel, who is an historical character, has been made one of the family of the Prinses, for the sake of the unity of the plot, but his actions, almost incredible as they appear, are not exaggerated.

The conversation of the female propaganda, the death-bed of the Marchioness, the preaching of the monk, the death of Rodolphe, the allusions to the Popes in the mouth of Malvicino, in short, well nigh every incident is based on facts, the principal exceptions being the development of the plot, properly so called, connected with Ardoine at the end of volume ii., and with Echard, volume iii.

These considerations, it is hoped, will add to the

value of the story. The author proposes a higher aim than enabling the thoughtless to get through the tedium of idleness—he is concerned with the propagation of truth. He has endeavoured to cast light on the false creed and acts of that mysterious Church, which is of a truth "drunk with the blood of the saints," and to illustrate those blessed truths which it is our glory to possess, and our responsibility to hand down, unimpaired, to our children. Above all he hopes that the truth of the Gospel will be found set forth in these pages, and that scenes like the death-beds of the Marchioness and of Marie will illustrate their respective principles and hopes.

The Waldenses are interesting to us, as forming the historic link between the Reformation and Apostolic times, having always protested against the innovations and heresies of the Church of Rome.

The author offers this mite as the contribution of an individual mind to what he believes to be the cause of truth, and as a protest against the encroachments of that Church, which, while she totters on the banks of the Tiber, is strengthening her stakes and lengthening her cords on the banks of the Thames.* Happy will he be if from his humble

---

* From 1850 to 1862 the *increase* of Romish priests in England and Scotland has been 459 (out of 1397) ; of chapels, 382 (out of 1065) ; of convents, 118 (out of 171).

parsonage he can promote the cause of truth, as the
Waldenses have done in the hidden valleys at the
base of Monte Viso.

With reference to the inevitable accusation of
partisan writing, he begs to observe that in times
such as those whereof he treats, the characters of
both parties become more defined and contrasted.
The rage and hatred of the persecutor thus serves
to develop the "patience and faith of the saints," and
a reference to any of the Histories of Persecutions
will prove that neither the one nor the other are
exaggerated, but that both phases are verified by
human experience.

As regards the charge of reviving "the evil"
which history has buried, we should remember that
the wisdom of the present is based upon the experience of the past; that so far from it being our duty,
in charity, to cast a veil over the crimes of the Romish Church, that arch conspirator against the liberties of mankind, it is a charity to the human race to
unmask their enemy, and to warn the present generation of the onslaught of an insidious foe.

The historical and oft-repeated crimes of a community like the Church of Rome (which appears to
be expressly denounced in the Word of God), and
the individual follies or errors of our neighbour,
require the exercise of a different charity. To be

blind to the latter may be a virtue; to be blind to the former must be a vice.

The author has but thrown the invectives and descriptions of general history into individual portraits, for what can exceed the horrors which Roman Catholic historians have left on record of the state of Ecclesiastical Society during the middle ages, and up to the time of which we write?

If systems of religion are to be judged by their fruits, Roman Catholicism has a long range of adverse testimonies from the Chairs of John XXIII., and of Alexander VI., through the zeal of Simon de Montfort, Dominic, Torquemada, or Pianesse, down to the laurelled warriors of Spoleto and the disloyal rabble of Cork.

Let us as Englishmen prize our blood-bought privileges, and by spiritual weapons resist the advance of that sect which hates freedom and only wants more power to rob us of earth's choicest birth-right, our civil and religious liberty.

A change, it is asserted, has of late come over the spirit of Rome; but in refutation of this, we may point to cases like that of Matamoros in Spain, and others, who were sentenced to eight and nine years of the galleys for reading the Scriptures. The Church of Rome professes to be infallible in doctrine, and persecution has been authorized and vindicated.

We do not say that all Roman Catholics are either intolerant or insincere, and we rejoice to do honour to Fenelon, Massillon, Guyon, Pascal, Samuel Vacca, and others of kindred spirit; but that the genius of the system is what we have represented, and that the characters of the time are not exaggerated, can be readily verified by appeals to authors of all persuasions.

With reference to the practices of Rome and her clergy in the present day, we may refer to the letter of Settembrini to Cardinal Riario Sforza, published in the *Times* of September 2, 1863. On such points let the Italians themselves be the judges. "In brief," writes the Cavalière Settembrini, "wherever we open the Gospel by accident, we see that the doctrine and the holy life of Jesus Christ are just the opposite of the doctrine of the Roman Catholic Church, and of the works of the priests."

The following is from a leading article in the *Times*, September 2, 1863 :—

"M. Montalembert throws the Inquisition overboard, and denounces the persecuting acts of the Roman Church. He sacrifices a whole page of the past. But this is not all that M. Montalembert does. He declares his hostility to all the existing remains of this system; to that modified persecution which consists in simply prohibiting the spread of new doctrines, and coercing the agents in such efforts, imprisoning them, and fining them. But this is the system now in Spain, it has only just been abolished by Sardinian rule in the greater part of Italy, and it is in full action at this moment in Rome. Anybody in the Papal states can be put in gaol for disseminating obnoxious doctrines."

The following quotation from Dr. Gilly will be read with interest:—

" Some of the narratives that I read seemed to give quite a romantic, and even fabulous air, to the conflicts which this little community (never exceeding twenty thousand souls) had the courage to hold with their powerful neighbours ; and my expectations were raised by several of the descriptions to see a region, which would appear more like fairy-land than the theatre of real achievements. Every vale and glen is represented in these relations as sacred ground, from having been ennobled by some exploit in defence of liberty or religion, or consecrated to the memory of a hero who had bled, or a martyr who had suffered there. One writer calls the valleys of these Vaudois 'an holy asylum which God has wonderfully and even miraculously fortified ;' and a Popish author, who wrote against the Vaudois, bears this remarkable testimony to their successful resistance of aggression. 'Toutes sortes de gens en divers temps, par un très-grand effort, ont en vain essayé de les arracher, car contre l'opinion de tout le monde ils sont toujours demeurez vainqueurs, et du tout invincibles.'*   But highly coloured as such accounts may be thought to be, an investigation into the history of these mountaineers, and a survey of their country, will clearly prove that neither the extraordinary events in the one, nor the beauty or sublimity described in the other, have been exaggerated.''

The author cannot refrain from quoting the following extract from Canon Wordsworth's speech in Convocation, February 12th, 1863 :—

"What could be a more wonderful thing than the fact that the very person—Father Carlo Passaglia—celebrated for his advocacy of the new doctrine of the Immaculate Conception, the very man who was especially honoured by Pope Pius IX., the man who had written three quarto volumes on behalf of that new doctrine, should be now residing at Turin, the capital of Piedmont, in the very house where Count Cavour was born, and where he died?   He had collected upwards of nine thousand signatures, all the signatures of priests contending for Italian liberty, and for the abolition of the temporal supremacy of the Pope.   Father Passaglia having, in the teeth of the anathemas of the Papacy, raised this cry for

* Claude Seyssel.

the abolition of the temporal supremacy, they must ultimately come to the question of the spiritual supremacy likewise. This manifestation against the temporal was also a protest against the spiritual supremacy. When they looked back to history, and remembered the horrors and massacres that were inflicted by the House of Savoy in the extermination of Christians, and when they now saw raised up an army of three hundred thousand men, combined with the voices of nine thousand priests in that very kingdom of Piedmont, under the rule of the ancient Duchy of Savoy, to recall the faithful to the very valleys of the Alps, they must acknowledge that the finger of God was in it :—

"'Avenge, O Lord, thy slaughtered saints, whose bones
Lie scattered on the Alpine mountains cold!'"

In order to give the reader some insight into the history of the time, the author subjoins the headings of the chapters of Dr. Muston's "Israel of the Alps," which refer to that period. (The most perfect list of books and manuscripts referring to this and other portions of the history of the Waldenses will be found at the end of Dr. Muston's second volume.)

CHAPTER VI.—THE PROPAGANDA (A.D. 1637 to A.D. 1655). — Charles Emmanuel II. of Savoy. — The Duchess Christina of France.—Disputes as to the Regency.—The Propaganda instituted.—Rorengo.—

1655).—The Fugitive Vaudois find an Asylum in the French Dominions.—Janavel, with a Small Band, obtains Wonderful Victories over the Troop of Pianesse.—Pianesse has recourse again to the Arts of Treachery.—He ravages Rora, but is attacked and defeated by Janavel as he retires with his Booty.—Pianesse marches against Rora with almost Ten Thousand Men.—Janavel's Wife and Daughter made Prisoners.—His Constant Resolutions.—The Duchess of Savoy and the French Court.—Mazarin refuses to take Part against the Vaudois as she desires.—Cromwell offers them a Refuge in Ireland.—Intercession of Foreign Powers.—Collections made for the Vaudois in Protestant Countries.—The Vaudois continue in Arms.—Another Vaudois Troop takes the Field under Jahier.—Janavel makes an attempt to seize Lucernette, but fails.—Jahier and he effects a Junction.—They seize St. Segont.—Further Successes.—Janavel is severely wounded.—Jahier is killed.

CHAPTER IX.—END OF THE CONFLICT, NEGOTIATIONS AND PATENTS OF GRACE (June to September 1655).—Foreigners come to the Assistance of the Vaudois.—Further Successes of their Arms.—They fail in an Attempt, conducted by the French General Descombies to take the Fort of La Tour.—Intervention of Cromwell.—His Ambassador Morland at Turin.—Treaty of Pignerol.

In conclusion, we joyfully acknowledge that a brighter day has of late dawned on Italy. The Vaudois have had their various civil disqualifications removed since 1848; they are now free Italians, having colleges at Florence and La Tour, and Churches and Evangelists in many parts of the Peninsula. May they become the Missionary Church of Italy! King Victor Emmanuel, by his enlightened policy, inherits their warmest loyalty, which even the persecutions of many of his ancestors failed to quench. Need we add that this liberty has been obtained by Romanists, not through, but *in spite* of the Church of Rome, which is the last nucleus of intolerance, despotism, and brigandism in this regenerated land.

Should any of his readers feel inclined to transmit their offerings in aid of this ancient yet struggling Church, the author will pledge himself for their due transmission. Commending his work to the blessing of the great Head of the Church, whose glory he would advance, the author concludes by wishing his readers the same pleasure and profit in the perusal of the following pages as he has had in his researches for their composition.

LATCHMOOR, GERRARD'S CROSS,
        January, 1864.

CONTENTS.

CONTENTS.

LIST OF ILLUSTRATIONS.

——◆——

MAP OF THE WALDENSIAN VALLEYS.

"Those who gave early notice, as the lark
    Springs from the ground the morn to gratulate,
    Who rather chose the day to antedate
    By striking out a solitary spark,
    When all the world with midnight gloom was dark;
    These harbingers of good, whom bitter hate
    In vain endeavour'd to exterminate,
    Fell obloquy pursues with hideous bark;
    But they desist not; and the sacred fire,
    Rekindled thus, from dens and savage woods
    Moves, handed on with never-ceasing care,
    Through courts, through camps, o'er limitary
        floods;
    Nor lacks this sea-girt isle a timely share
    Of the new flame, nor suffer'd to expire."

                                    Wordsworth.

VOL. I.

THE VALLEYS.

AD LECTOREM.

THE reader is particularly requested to peruse attentively the Preface and the Appendix at the end of each Volume, and if curiously-minded to verify the quotations, by reference to the originals.

N.B.—The Vaudois and Waldenses are synonymous terms; they are Italians, inhabiting the Alpine valleys of Piedmont, and must not be confounded with the Swiss of the Pays de Vaud, in Switzerland.

THE

SIX SISTERS OF THE VALLEYS.

CHAPTER I.

THE PALACE.

ANNO DOMINI 1655. It is the first of January, a day, breathing with the mystic eloquence of time, fraught with the memories of the past, the enjoyment of the present, and the chequered hopes and fears of the undeciphered future.

The lonely peasant on yon mountain range has watched with untutored eagerness for the early sunrise, and when at length the sudden glitter of a distant point across the dreary plain assures him that another year has really dawned, his heart partakes the common impulse of joy that thrills the human race.

VOL. I.   B

The glow of the southern sun waxes brighter, and the outline of a colossal cupola, surmounted by that glittering point, becomes more distinct. It overlooks a city in which past and present mingle in strange contrast, and whose discordant buildings embody the collisions of rival ages.

Here stands the gorgeous church, redolent with incense; there the roofless temple, with its orphan columns, and its voiceless shrine : on one side of a street rises the marble palace, adorned with modern heraldry; while on the other lies a broken frieze, its fragments strewn along the pathway: on this spot stands a gallery of art, opposite to which a Corinthian capital juts from the ground, or is embedded in modern brickwork : at this point the thronged bridge spans the tawny river, while close by, the dismantled arch of victory, ravaged by centuries, protests, in its silent decay, against man's fancied immortality on earth.

From these broken shrines Wisdom utters her parable.

The up-heaved stones which kings once reared, the rifled sepulchres of the nameless dead, warn the thoughtless crowd who trample upon their fathers' ashes, that they too will soon be consigned to the remorseless grave, themselves trackless and forgotten.

It was still early in the morning, when an aged and decrepid man stepped into one of the balconies of a large, irregular pile of building, which stood in the outskirts of the city. His dim eye was brightened for a moment, as he felt his flagging energies revived by the elastic morning air. From his peculiar style of dress, he appeared to be a person of ecclesiastical rank; he was clothed in a white woollen robe, upon which was embroidered a large cross, partially concealed by the overhanging cape; his grey locks straggled from under a small white cap closely fitting the crown of his head, and his wrinkled face bore evident traces of care and mental conflict, despite an expression of sensuality and indolence. Gazing into the heavens with a look of vacancy, he watched the fragments of fleecy clouds floating athwart the otherwise unbroken azure; then, recalled by the morning chimes of the neighbouring churches, he turned his eye upon the city spread out before him, vainly hoping that earth might diffuse that peace which heaven seemed to have denied.

The scene was one which might cause the most thoughtless to reflect, for of all the cities of the earth none has exercised a greater influence on the political or religious destinies of the human race than this, the imperial city of Rome. That feeble man was its sovereign, and well might he pause as he beheld the centre of his spiritual and temporal power. His eye catches a glimpse of the classic river winding along, banked by structures, ancient and modern, dimly outlined in the dusky wave. Conspicuous

in the foreground stands a round castellated
building, at once a fortress, a prison, and a
tomb ; to the right rises a dome, open to the
sunshine and rain of heaven; while farther
yet is another relic of antiquity, a large
circular fragment towering aloft, pierced
with tiers of arches, through which the
distant landscape can be dimly traced.

On the blank plains beyond are lines of
arched masonry converging to the city,
now an unbroken length, now rent in
twain, standing on the desert in solemn
silence, steeped with the history of a past
race who brought from the mountain glen,
into the city's midst, the priceless stream.
In the distance arise the shadowy mountains, forming a contrast with their purple
bases and silvery summits to the dark
blue sky, and varying in their thousand
tints as they are mellowed by the cloudless or clouded sun.

The old man surveyed the scene,
closing his eyes from time to time as if to

follow the current of his troubled thoughts.
This was Pope Innocent X. His withered
hand, upon which shone a magnificent
ring, grasped a parchment covered with
black letters and illuminated capitals, and
bearing a small seal of lead stamped on
one side with the heads of Peter and Paul,
and on the other, with the words "Innocent VIII. Pont. Max. An. III." This
ancient record was the famous Bull of
1487, issued for the extirpation of heresy,
more especially that phase which clung so
tenaciously to the fastnesses of the Alps,
and the plains of Languedoc, Dauphiny,
and Provence. The fulminations of that
parchment had produced a baneful effect
on superstitious Europe. Thousands,
whose sins were as scarlet, joined the
crusade in hope of expiating their crimes,
and securing an indisputable right to the
kingdom of God, by shedding innocent
blood.

Eight hundred thousand Protestants,

it is recorded, perished in different parts of Europe.

Nearly. two centuries had rolled over since that time, and though the originators of that bloody drama had passed away, their principles unhappily survived.

A cloud had arisen once more in the horizon, and the year 1655 opened gloomily for the primitive churches in the valleys of the Alps.

After glancing at the document, Innocent retired into his chamber, and seating himself began to read:—

"*Innocentius Episcopus, servus servorum Dei, dilecto Filio, Alberto de Capitaneis.*"

The old man paused as he uttered his predecessor's name. Breathing heavily he continued:—

"*Non sine displicentiâ grandi pervenit auditumque quod nonnulli iniquitatis filii, incolæ Provinciæ Ebredumensis, sectatores illius perniciosissimæ et abominabilis sectæ*

*hominum malignorum, Pauperum de Lugduno
seu Valdensium, nuncupatorum, quæ dudum
in partibus Pedemontanis,"* . . . . . .

The Pontiff's feeble voice gradually
became more indistinct, and he dozed off
into a broken sleep.

After some time several acolytes entered
the room, and having awakened his Holiness, conducted him to the Sala Regia,
where upon New Year's-day he was accustomed to give audience to the ambassadors
of foreign courts.   The hall was spacious,
and gorgeously decorated with stucco ornaments and frescoes.   One group represented
Gregory VII. giving absolution to the Emperor Henry IV.; another, Frederick Barba-
rossa, receiving the blessing of Alexander
III.   On the eastern side Vasari's master-
piece attracted a crowd of admirers.   The
painter might well illustrate the subject,
for it had caused the bells of St. Peter to
ring, the cannon of St. Angelo to thunder,
bonfires to blaze in the streets of Rome,

and the founders at the mint to strike a new medal. Let us approach the picture. It portrays not the struggle of battle, and yet those ghastly forms bespeak the riot of death. The sword is raised aloft dripping with blood; the young man is hewn down and breathes his last, clasping the body of his aged father; the loving and fragile beauty is murdered within sight of her husband's corpse; and the tender babe is dashed against the stones. Fury goads the pursuers; the agony of death thrills the victim. This is Rome's offering of a sweet-smelling savour to a God of love, who came on earth not to destroy men's lives, but to save them.

Behold this work of art on the walls of the Vatican, accredited in the palace of Christ's so-called Vicar on earth, lingering to this day to testify of the past. It represents the massacre of St. Bartholomew;—alas! only one item out of the roll of massacres due to parchments sealed with

the fisherman's seal. It is the unconscious
epitaph of sixty thousand Protestants who
perished in France alone. On receiving the
details, Gregory XIII. cried out aloud,
" Good news! Good news!" St. Peter's
rang with the hymn of St. Ambrose, " *Te
Deum Laudamus.*" A medal was struck
with the inscription, " *Ugonotorum Strages,*
1572," and the invention of art was en-
listed that the damnable crime might be
graven on the Church's brow.

At the upper end of the hall was a
richly decorated throne, on the back of which
two keys crossed, surmounted by a triple
crown, were embroidered in gold. A file of
the noble guard was ranged on either side
of the hall, who presented their swords and
fell on bended knee as the sovereign Pontiff
passed them. Having ascended the throne
he bent his head, and after a pause said
aloud, in a peculiar cadence, " *Dominus
vobiscum,*" and stretching out two fingers
of his right hand, made a motion, at which

the beholders fell on their knees and crossed themselves. In the centre of the hall the ambassadors of most of the courts of Europe were grouped with ecclesiastics of various orders. France, Spain, Portugal, Austria, Naples, and minor duchies are represented. In the front stands a subtle, black-eyed man, whose outward garb betokens no rank. He is general of the order of Jesuits. Near him an older man wears the robe of the Dominican. Franciscans and hooded Capuchins intermingle with Carmelites, Benedictines, and Cistercians, while contrasting with the sombre garb of the ecclesiastics appear the varied uniforms of generals and officers, many of whose breasts glitter with orders and stars. Cardinals, with red hats and purple mantles, are grouped in knots earnestly discussing the health of Innocent, and the probable vacancy of St. Peter's chair. One by one the audience approach the sovereign Pontiff; some salute his hand, others his knee, while those of inferior grade kneel and touch with their lips his embroidered slipper.

After several had been presented, a young officer entered, wearing the uniform of the Duke of Savoy. An ingenuous expression lit up his flashing eye and regular features, which contrasted favourably with the cunning selfishness visible in the countenances of many of those around. He paused before the Holy Father's throne, and bent his knee :—

"Son," said the old man, "tell our beloved Charles Emmanuel and his mother Christina that we commend their works of love, and send them and all who labour with them our Apostolic blessing. We thank God," said he, as his voice trembled through weakness, "that the jubilee of 1650 has brought forth such good fruit in the establishment of the Holy Office at Turin. We have studied the Bull of our predecessor, Innocent VIII. (whose soul God rest in

peace), in which he urges the Christian
world to the extermination of heresy. We
approve of the measures our beloved daughter of Savoy intends taking for the uprooting of those ancient rebels in the valleys of
the Alps. Bid her purify her kingdom and
win an eternal crown; let the sword support the cross, and the cross will hallow
the sword. Look, young man, at that picture; stamp it on your memory for ever; it
is the triumph of the Church over her apostate children, whom she would convert
even by the sword. Would that all our
sons would follow this bright example, and
emulate the zeal of the eldest son of the
Church! Our age would not then be so
barren in works of faith and labours of love.
Accept this sword, whose blade is of our
best Ferrara steel, and upon whose jewelled handle our pontifical arms are wrought.
May it recal to you the scenes of the Eternal
City; may it prove trusty in the hour of
danger; and remind you of your allegiance

to our Most Holy See. Fear not to use it
at the Church's bidding for the conversion
of heretics. Take these presents to the Duke
and Regent; assure them of our fatherly prayers, and convey our Apostolic benediction."

The officer arose, and, bowing three
times, retreated backwards from the presence of Innocent. After a few other audi-
ences the Holy Father was carried to his
private room, traversing a long corridor
lined with the choicest efforts of ancient
art, and draped with the tapestries of
Raphael. Little cared he then for these
monuments of the past; his strength was
ebbing, and his mind jaded, for all this outward pomp veiled a conscience ill at ease
with itself and with God.

Later in the day he passed through the
same hall, into the adjoining apartments.
The throne of state, the golden crucifix
on the altar, the exquisite candelabra,
the work of Cellini, the carved stalls of
the choir, indicated that it was the

Sistine chapel. The walls were covered with frescoes, while in the panels between the windows were portraits of various popes; on the ceiling was the master-piece of Michael Angelo, "The Last Judgment," the execution of which had occupied the great artist for a period of eight years. The aged pontiff seemed to be labouring under the most agonizing feelings; he cast himself on his face before the high altar, where he remained motionless for some minutes; rising, he moved about with trembling step; now he seated himself on that throne on which he had sat not many days before on the festival of the Nativity; anon he wandered among the stalls of the choir, and coming back within the rails, knelt on the steps of the altar; but he found no rest.

"What!" he cried aloud, as he gazed aloft at the solemn frescoes which he could just discern in the declining day, "Is there no peace of conscience for me? Can I dispense pardon and salvation to thousands, and yet not minister to my own diseased mind? Why is this retrospect of my past life forced upon me? Why is my conscience like a hell within my breast? Accursed Olympia! would that I had never known thee! I have sinned like Herod; ah! worse than Herod, and now my broken vows, and the stings of past crime, are crushing my very soul."

"O God!" he exclaimed, after a pause, as he shook his grey hairs, and trampled under foot his white cap, "I have read of the agonies of conscience, but now I feel them."

The wretched man fell down upon the steps; he stretched out his hands as if convulsively grasping at something, while the broken words fell from him—

"Have mercy on me!—Avaunt, Olympia! Jansenius—did I condemn him?—In how many points—five,—five?—Do they say that I am infallible in matters

of doctrine and not in matters of fact?
—Why will the Jesuits assail me?—
What! will they fight the Jansenists?—
Who am I—a Pamfili?—Avaunt, Olympia!
Mal-dachini.—My brother's widow; I hate
thee now.—How many bishopricks hast
thou given away?—Avaunt, I say!—Have
mercy on me!—*Kyrie Eleison. Maria, Regina Angelorum.*"—

For some time his eyes remained fixed,
as if gazing into vacancy; then a paroxysm
of grief seemed to give relief, and his
scalding tears fell on the marble steps.
Again the solemn silence was broken by
loud cries—"*Sancta Maria—Janua Cœli*—
have mercy on me."

His strength then ebbing, he rolled off
the steps, and lay prostrate on the pavement, gasping for breath—a sad spectacle of
the frailty and wickedness of human nature,
and more revolting when we discern in this
conscience-stricken culprit him who falsely
claimed the power of the keys.

A few days after this, Innocent took to his bed, and on the seventh of the same month sank under the load of care and old age. So selfish were his relations, whom he had enriched out of the coffers of the church, that none were willing to pay his funeral expenses. For three days the wretched corpse lay neglected in the palace of the church, without the ordinary decencies of Christian mourning, until a canon, who had been once in the papal service, expended a small sum, and caused the last honours to be rendered to his late master.

CHAPTER II.

OUR scene is changed from central to northern Italy. We are in the Cottian Alps, a section of the mighty vertebræ of Europe, situated about thirty miles west of Turin, and about seventy south of Mont Blanc. Among these mountains lie hidden the three world-renowned valleys of Lucerna, St. Martin, and Perouse, the immemorial sanctuaries of the Waldensian Church.

At the foot of the giant spur which forms one side of the valley of Lucerna, and trends upwards, until it terminates in Monte Viso, was the farm of La Baudènc. Its arrangement was quadrangular, one

still common in the north of Italy. Two
sides of the square were composed of
the dwelling-rooms of the family, divided
into two stories, round the upper of which
ran a wooden gallery, looking into the court-
yard. The third side consisted of a row of
out-buildings, roughly covered with flags
of mica-schist, supported by arched pillars,
behind which various implements of household and agricultural use were mingled with
stacks of firewood, casks, churns, and carts,
among which the young children were wont
to amuse themselves by chasing each other.
On the fourth side was a large gateway opening on to the lane, leading to the main road
from La Tour to Pignerol. The approach
was covered with a wooden trellis work,
which was now bare, but in summer it
formed a delightful rustic avenue, when the
festooned vines, shaded by the chestnuts
and walnuts, tempered the heat of the
Italian sun, and with their hanging clusters
suggested the idea of peace and plenty.

Under this one roof dwelt the family of Prins. It consisted of six brothers, who, having married six sisters, had, notwithstanding their respective marriages, continued to live together without division of property, and without discord. In this singular union of two families, the eldest brother of the one had married the eldest sister of the other, and they were recognized as the common father and mother of the little colony, while the other members of the household had their allotted spheres of labour among the cattle, in the meadows, or in the vineyards.

Those relations so common in the pages of fiction, so rare in actual life, were realized in this extraordinary and patriarchal family. The threat of separation was never heard among them, each successive marriage having, contrary to proverbial experience, served only to widen an unbroken circle of affection and common interest. The household, including the children, numbered upwards of forty persons; forming, in that thinly inhabited country, a community in itself.

Rodolphe, the aged father of the sisters, was still alive. He was held in the greatest respect throughout the valleys, having been formerly, for many years, pastor at La Tour, and Moderator of the Waldensian churches. Janavel, the eldest brother, was a good specimen of the dauntless mountaineer. Reared under the shadow of the eternal Alps, he possessed those high qualities which are found only among the uncorrupted sons of nature. The most childlike simplicity was blended in his eagle eye, with that piercing glance which reads the secret motives of an adversary's heart. Reliant upon God, and referring with unquestioning submission to his Word and will, there was no danger which he dared not challenge in the path of duty, supported more by his unwavering faith, than by the promptings of his natural courage. The general superintendence of the farm, with the special management of the vineyards, was assigned to him, in conjunction with his son Raynald. His wife Martha, the eldest of the sisters, was remarkable for her expression of settled melancholy, which could not fail to strike the most unobservant. The garb of mourning which she habitually wore offered a strange contrast to her pallid cheek, and her countenance was shaded by a pensiveness evidently due to heartfelt sorrow. Her husband treated her grief with respect and tenderness, never interfering with its manifestation, nor chiding her for its long continuance, knowing that it had become a second nature and a mournful pleasure.

Martha was accustomed to preside at the common table. At her right hand was placed an empty chair, towards which the mother cast occasional glances, and which even the little Claude never presumed to occupy. Daily at sunset she retired to her chamber for prayer, and when she rejoined her sisters her dark eyes bore traces of grief, and her cheeks the stain of tears.

At a certain season the cloud upon her brow grew darker. Martha then clung with the increased intensity of a mother's love to her son Raynald, in whose sympathy she confided, and to whose prayers she listened, until peace was restored to her mind, and the temptation to arraign the dispensations of God subdued within her sorrowing soul.

Raynald was in his twenty-sixth year. In physical appearance he was of Herculean mould. Tall, but well proportioned, he excelled in feats of personal daring, and was the acknowledged champion in all athletic exercises of strength and courage. But though nature had been lavish of her outward gifts, she had not, in his case, made them the substitute for those higher qualities of the mind, intelligence and delicacy of feeling. He was impulsive in temper, but affectionate in heart, and partaking the natural simplicity of his father's character, was tender and thoughtful in his attentions to his mother and aunts. Having been for some time impressed with personal religion he contemplated becoming a pastor, a prospect which afforded partial consolation to his mother in her settled grief.

David and Lucille were the second couple of this singular family. Martha had resigned the household *ménage* as irksome in her state of mind, and the light-hearted Lucille fulfilled its duties to the satisfaction of all. Thoughtful of others, thoughtless of herself, Lucille cared not what labour she undertook for the benefit of her friends. Her matronly face was brightened with a smile when she met the younger children in the court, and she would rarely pass them without slipping a chestnut or some other acceptable trifle into their hands.

The management of the flocks was confided to Marguerite and Madeleine, who were seldom apart, save when their own families required the mother's care. Theirs was the love of sisters, a love like that of the mother, the admiration of every age for its guileless purity, lingering in the heart as a faint memory of Eden. Though they were twins they did not resemble each other in person nor character. Marguerite had raven hair, a dark, flashing eye, lips which could express scorn when her lofty spirit brought a cloud over her Grecian features. The severe intellectual was her delight, and as in early life she had received instruction in the dead languages from her father, she was well qualified to be the companion of her husband Jean, whose timid and studious disposition led him to shun the whirl of daily life.

Madeleine was the reverse of her sister. Apt to rely upon Marguerite from her youth, she possessed the clinging qualities of the ivy rather than the self-sustaining power of the oak. She was in heart what

Marguerite was in head, and the union of the two would have formed a perfect character. Even after her marriage Madeleine clung to Marguerite with undiminished fervour, and having lately become a widow, the life-long devotion had assumed that sanctity which can be felt only by a desolate heart, merging itself into one absorbing object for sympathy and consolation.

Every evening she repaired to her sister's room to hear the experiences of the day, and to enjoy that bright fellowship of feeling which is the privilege of earth and the birthright of heaven.

The husband of Renée was Daniel, to whom the care of the meadows and the tillage of the fields were allotted.

Marie was the sixth sister, but as we shall revert more particularly to her, we shall take her daughter, Ardoine, as her representative in the family group.

Ardoine was about two and twenty, having been born shortly before the commencement of her mother's illness. She was of a northern rather than a southern type. She had not the black hair, the dark eye, the sunburnt tint of the Italian; her complexion was fair, her hair of a golden hue, her long tresses knotted behind with the carelessness of innocence, and of unconscious beauty. Although her features might not be called regular, there was something in the sweetness of her expression which more than atoned for any deviation from the strict lines of beauty. Her eye shone not so much with the fire of intelligence as with the soft subduing power of goodness. It was the eye of a woman, and woman is the gem of nature, and the eye the gem of woman. Who knows not the magic power of the chasing phases of the eye—that speck on which the Almighty hath emblazoned his triple attributes of wisdom, power, and goodness; that point, on which a landscape is engraven from without, or the subtle spirit imaged from within? Her eyes were the interpreters of her soul; they spake of tenderness and love, the twin instincts of the true woman's heart. They were generally radiant with unselfish joy, but soon became shaded with the film of sorrow when a sister's grief demanded a sympathetic tear. They were such as are seen but once in a lifetime, and when seen are never forgotten, touching as they do the inner springs of life, a feat wrought only by the eloquence of nature. What wonder then that they made an impression on Raynald, and caused his impulsive heart to tremble when their eyes unconsciously met!

Ardoine had long been under religious convictions. Impressed with the truths she had learned from her grandfather, she endeavoured to consecrate her most trivial act by the sublimity of Christian motive, the glory of God.

When any one happened to express a wish, Ardoine noted it; the little kind-

ness was done in silence, and the aunt
or cousin would gratefully find the deed of
love rendered by an unknown hand.   From
the time when, as a child, she played under
the village chestnut, her name had been a
household word in the valley of Lucerna,
and in the châlets of Angrogna the young
shepherds sang tributes to her worth.

Such, with the addition of the various
groups of children of every age, was the
family of Prins at the period when our
narrative commences, the first day of
January, 1655.

CHAPTER III.

IN a large vaulted room, whose sides were covered with wainscoting, were gathered a band of children, eleven or twelve in number, ranging from four to ten years of age. Their sparkling eyes and joyous smiles bespoke the buoyancy of innocence and health. A little boy, the centre of the group, was taking upon himself the office of marshalling the band. His light hair and ruddy cheeks contrasted pleasantly with the dark eyes and darker complexions of many of his cousins.

"Come, Susanne," said the lad, "this is New Year's Day; now are we all ready?

We must go to grandfather first, and wish him a happy new year. I hope we all know our texts perfectly, so that he may give us one of his kind smiles when he hears us repeat them without missing a word."

" Etienne," replied Susanne, her eyes brightening as she spoke, " I think I know mine ; I repeated it over six times to myself in bed last night."

" And I am sure I ought to know mine," said little Lena, " for cousin Ardoine took me on her knee yesterday, and said it over to me such a number of times, and I repeated it word for word after her till I could say it alone."

" And do you remember your speech of good wishes to your good grandpapa, my little Aline ?"

" Yes, cossy Ardy told me to say, May the sun shine on your grey hair all the year, grandpa."

" And you, cousin André, what have you got to repeat ?"

"Ardoine has given me a verse. She said it was made up of short words, and was very beautiful. 'The Son of Man is come to seek and to save that which was lost.' But I wanted to learn more, and have another. 'God is love. We love him because he first loved us.'"

"And here is my brother Claude. Has our good, kind sister taught him anything?"

"'God bless papa. Praise God.'"

"Very well," said the little marshal; "now join hands two and two, and when you come into grandfather's room, make your bows, and say your speeches one after the other."

The children arranged themselves in pairs. Etienne surveyed the group, and being satisfied with his inspection, put himself at its head. Having knocked at his grandfather's door, he opened it and ushered in his band with all due form.

Here sat the aged patriarch in his arm-chair, his snow-white hair streaming

over his shoulders, his mild and clear
eyes beaming with an expression of bene-
volence. On the table lay his open Bible,
the guide of his youth, the solace of his
declining years, and of whose glorious
truths he had been for so many years a
fervid preacher. His eye glistened when
he beheld the loved procession enter. Some
of the fathers and mothers gathered round
his chair, looking on with smiles mingled
with tears, while Ardoine standing in the
background, peeped, from time to time,
over her grandfather's shoulder, at the little
company, and anxiously listened how they
would acquit themselves.

Up toddled the first pair, and made
their bow. Susanne, standing on the
right, was the first to speak.

" ' Well done, good servant ; enter thou
into the joy of thy Lord.' "

Then followed Bertin. " ' The Lord
bless thee, and keep thee from this time
forth for evermore.' "

Susanne added, "May the blessing of a little child fall sweetly on an old man ! "

Madeleine, whose head leaned on Marguerite's shoulder, clasped her sister, as her little one stood before her father, for those simple words caused the pure heart of the mother to yearn.

"Sister," whispered she, "I hope you are pleased with your godchild, she will be sure to have a text for you."

"Hush! my Bertin is now speaking; how nicely he holds your Susy's hand."

"The gratitude of a united family," said the boy, "make thy latter days brighter than thy youth."

The blessing of childhood, so plaintive to the aged, caused a tear to glisten in Rodolphe's eye, and his breast heaved with a half suppressed sigh, as the voices of infancy awoke the dormant memories of his own father and mother, and of his boyhood's home.

Placing his right hand on Bertin's head

and his left on that of Susanne, he gently said, "'The God who hath fed me all my life long, the Angel which redeemed me from all evil, bless the children.'" The others, having repeated their verses, knelt round him in a circle.

Rodolphe's lips moved as if in secret prayer, then placing his hands on each in turn, he blessed them in the name of his father's God. The scene was one instinct with the sacredness of family ties, and deeply affecting to the beholders, who saw old age and childhood thus blended, the one finishing, the other commencing its earthly pilgrimage.

"And now, my children," said the aged patriarch, "I ought to reply to your kind wishes, and make my New Year's speech. Susanne, may the tears which your mother shall shed over you, be those of joy and not of grief! Bertin, may you be good rather than clever, and the same son to your father that he has been to me!

Children," continued he, looking up at his sons and daughters, " children, elder and younger, how great is the goodness of God ! This day we enter on another year. Who can tell what may happen during its course ? We know not what a day may bring forth, or whether we shall be spared to meet together at its close. The present times are troublous ; our church has been a living witness for God's truth in this place from time immemorial, and we may expect suffering for the trial of our faith, even as they have persecuted our fathers in times past. Children," pursued Rodolphe, in a tone of solemn feeling, "as one whose voice shall soon be silent in the grave, as one who stands on the brink of eternity, over whose head have passed more than fourscore years, I say to you, should the dreadful trial ever come that you are called upon to renounce your faith, choose suffering before abjuration, death rather than apostasy. Never flinch from the true gospel of grace.

Remember that he who loves lands, or
children, or life, better than Christ, is not
worthy of Him.   He is the treasure of
earth and heaven, whom it is blessed to
follow even at the loss of all things.
Kneel, my sons and daughters, let me
bless you once again, lest we all meet
together no more on earth."

The married couples then knelt where
their children had just been kneeling, and
bowed their heads before their aged father.
The same thin hand was placed on each, and
the same gentle voice breathed that blessing
which was the right and privilege of age
and virtue to grant.

Janavel and the pensive Martha knelt
side by side, followed by their grown-up
daughters, and, at some distance, by the
athletic Raynald, who had edged a little
out of his place in order to approach
Ardoine.   David and Lucille rank next to
Jean and Marguerite, each couple surrounded by its respective group.   Made-

leine is alone, for she is a widow; Renée
comes next with Daniel. The sixth sister is
absent; it is Marie, who languishes on her
bed. But she and her lost husband are
represented by their daughter Ardoine.
She knelt for some time in silence before
her grandfather, who, placing both his
hands on her head, looked up to heaven
and breathed a double blessing upon her,
who had no father to bless his child.

As Rodolphe bent low, his silvered hair
appeared whiter from contrast with those
golden locks upon which his shrivelled
hand rested so long.

Bright was this moral union of age and
beauty. In purity of faith, and excellence
of character, that grandfather and grand-
daughter were one. A friendship, guileless as that which angels feel for good men,
knit them together. What, if among the
loved, she was the beloved of that old man!
Whose was the first morning welcome
which sounded in his ear? Who knew his

little ways and anticipated his wants?
Who opened his book at its accustomed
place and laid on the page the fresh mountain flower? Who ran to bring him the
glass of bright cold water from the spring,
dear to him from its association with his
boyhood? It was Ardoine. Well might
his hand rest long upon that daughter's
head, and the father's heart flush once
more with the glow of nature's love.

"Come, little ones," said Etienne, after
his parents had risen, "say good-bye to
grandfather. You know where we must go
next."

"Oh, to aunty Marie, I shall be so glad
to see her, for I love her," said little
Aline.

"Then make your bow, and let us go."

So off they went, a blithe band, upon
whom youth had as yet dawned brightly,
and who knew neither the cares of life nor
the griefs which whiten the hair. But even
the least of them felt instinctively the

sympathy of suffering, for their little prattle
waxed softer, and their tones became more
subdued, as they proceeded to the chamber
of the invalid.

"Aunt Marie," said Etienne, on entering, "I have brought my little company
this New Year's morning, and hope you will
be able to listen to them for a short time.
Speak gently, dears, so as to disturb aunt
as little as possible."

Again did the little speech-makers
come forward in turn, and repeat the
verses already uttered in the hearing of
their grandfather, with some slight varia-
tion in the expression of their good
wishes.

The scene was changed, but its moral
suggestions were the same. Bright-eyed
infancy was in contact, not with old age,
but with suffering. The afflicted aunt had
been imprisoned in that chamber, years before the eldest of that band was born.
They had come into the world—their

powers were expanding, their youth and
strength were freshening, but in place
and circumstances she had remained the
same.

The children looked with affection on
that pale face, and kissed that shadowy
hand, as it lay on the coverlet of the
couch.

"God bless you, my dear ones,"
whispered Marie; "how good God is to
let me have such a refreshment of spirit,
and to learn how 'Out of the mouths of
babes and sucklings he can perfect praise.'"

Advancing two and two the children
knelt by the bedside.

The invalid laid her right hand on each
of them in turn, but the movement was
painful, and her voice was low, as she whispered her blessing.

Ardoine stood at the foot of the bed,
gazing on that pale countenance with
the devotion of duty and pity, and the
tear dimmed that bright blue eye when

she remembered her parent's absence from that family band. Guessing her mother's wishes, Ardoine brought out some cakes of Indian corn, mixed with currants, and, with a loving smile, gave one to each of the children.

"Mother," said Ardoine, later in the afternoon, as she stooped over the bed and kissed her pale cheek, "I trust this morning's scene has not been too much for you; we could none of us be content without wishing you a happy New Year, and receiving your blessing; and the children would have been disappointed if they could not have come to you."

"God bless you, my daughter, and reward you a thousand-fold for your unfailing love towards your suffering mother; but I hear steps on the stairs, and they sound like those of Raynald."

"I am so glad for your sake, mother," replied Ardoine, "for he is so kind to you, and you are always so pleased to see him."

"And are not you my daughter?" said Marie, with a faint smile.

Ardoine had no time to reply, for at this moment the door opened, and Raynald entered.

CHAPTER IV.

THE SIXTH SISTER.

ADJOINING the chambers set apart for the use of the family, was a small outbuilding abutting on one side of the quadrangle— part of the main dwelling, and yet virtually a detached house, having two entrances, one from the inner court, and the other from the outside. In a room of this outbuilding lay the sixth sister, Marie. She had been carried to the chamber of sickness twenty-one years before, and had never since descended the narrow staircase. On first beholding her a stranger could hardly resist feeling surprise and fear. Was she alive? No sound, no motion, betrayed the lurking consciousness. The peculiar hue of death was stamped upon her face. The unearthly pallor, the closed eye, the motionless form, the solemn stillness, all seemed to be the external proofs of death, and it was difficult to believe that life lingered in that apparent corpse. The silence of the sick-room resembled that of the grave, for it was only on approaching the sufferer that her painful breathing became audible. The curtained window restrained the strong glare of day, diffusing a subdued light which augmented the solemnity of feeling produced by the scene. Her dark hair presented the only contrast to her blanched cheek, and seemed to belie the ravages of her disease. The expression upon her countenance was one of calm triumph, arising from a mind at peace with God and in charity with man. On a nearer approach the traces of premature age and protracted suffering became visible, yet these were swept away when she dilated

on the subject which absorbed her heart,
and at the name of Jesus her face was
brightened as with the smile of health.
Her illness had a melancholy origin. During one of those minor persecutions to
which the Waldenses were subject, she had
been cast into a dungeon in the castle of
Lucerna. She lingered there for six weeks,
with the damp pavement as her only
bed, and without change of raiment.
Though no actual mutilations had been
inflicted, yet she had been subjected to a
species of mental torture which is the re-
finement of cruelty. The soldiers who were
on guard battered at the door incessantly,
so that continuous sleep became an im-
possibility, and terrified her with accounts
of the torments she might suffer if she
refused to go to mass. After six weeks'
torture in the pestilent prison, fever
supervened, and as her death was considered certain she was cast out into the
woods of Lucerna, where she was acci-

dentally rescued by one of her father's flock. Exposure, fever, and horror had undermined her nervous energies, and left their cruel impress on her impaired constitution. She entered the dungeon in the glow of health, she came out a living corpse. From that time varied diseases had battled in her frame. Her tremulous breath seemed a direct loan from heaven, and she lay supported by pillows, expecting every moment to be her last.

All were touched on beholding this wreck of suffering, due to the persecuting hand of man. But the stranger's sympathy soon ebbed into admiration when mind came into collision with mind, and she divulged the latent consolations that possessed her soul. Her unruffled peace and stable joy were a moral prodigy. She gloried in tribulation, and was not weary of the Lord's correction. Like the sand, which ages ago was so soft as to receive the impress of the passing shower, and though

hardened into the massive rock still retains
unimpaired the delicacy of its former impressions, so with her responsive soul,
every pain, every sigh, was producing its
effect in tracing thereon more accurately
the image of God, preparatory to its eternal
maintenance. From her lips nothing was
common-place, for the most threadbare
maxim received emphasis from the lip of
suffering, as well as that charm which only
the living voice can convey; more touch-
ingly amid the silence of the sick-room.

The furniture around the bed was of
the scantiest description; a wardrobe and
a sofa, on which lay a Bible, a few books,
and knitting implements. The floor was
partially covered with a strip of carpet
brought by Raynald from the valleys of
France, which gave relief to the faded
curtains of the couch.

In this chamber, eleven years before,
Marie's husband had breathed his last.
The husband and the wife had lain side by

side on that bed of sickness, the one hover-
ing for years on the brink of the grave ;
the other prostrated in the vigour of manhood.

Happily they were able to reciprocate
the experiences of faith, and to strengthen
each other in the name of their Redeemer.

It was a melancholy duty for Ardoine
to minister to her parents, painfully doubting which of them she might lose first.
Contrary to expectation, the last was first,
and the first last. Marie, who had already
undergone ten years of excruciating suffering, was destined to linger for more than
another decade.

As might be naturally expected, she
was an object of special interest to the
whole of that loving circle.

Rodolphe paid her a daily visit. Bent
with years and leaning on his staff, he
entered that room to interchange thought
and feeling with another who, like himself,
was on the confines of the grave.

The voice of the father sounded sweetly in the daughter's ear as he spake of Christ, his hope and glory, while the faint whispers of the daughter echoed with equal sweetness in the ear of the aged father, for neither pain nor age had numbed in either the instincts of nature. They would converse for hours on experimental religion. Shut out from the routine of life, and having gradually lost her eyesight, Marie's memory recurred to those passages of Scripture which she had learned in youth—they came molten from a suffering heart, partaking the same spirit which had often dictated the words. To grasp these phases of truth, the father, though all his life a preacher of the Gospel, sat at the feet of his child, for the experiences of suffering cannot be learned by theory from the volumes of theology. The other five sisters would daily minister to the invalid, soothing her spirit in the way most natural to their individual dispositions. Martha turned to those passages of Scripture which spake of mental conflict and sorrow, and thus she struck a chord in unison with Marie's state of mind. Lucille, whose buoyant disposition led her to look joyfully on life, turned to those bright visions of the future enrapturing to her heart and fancy.

Renée would take a portion of the Psalms, and in her plaintive voice hymn them to some familiar tune which recalled the memory of bygone days. Marguerite delighted to dwell on the Epistle to the Hebrews. Being of a reflective mind, she loved to trace the apostle's chain of reasoning, and thus instructed her sister, whose sufferings reacted on the skilled interpreter ; while Madeleine sat at her feet, and equally with Marie drank in her words, now and then gently asking some question for further information. Ardoine, always bright and lively, never thinking of the pleasures that attract young people, would have been chained to that bedside, had not obedience

and duty required her to consider her own
health. The mother felt that influence of
love, and the dreamless hours of the night
would glide by more swiftly when she knew
that her child was sleeping near her couch.
There was a tenderness in all the daughter
did. The very cup of cold water was
priceless in her hand, enhanced by a winning
speech or smile of love. Ardoine shone in
that sick-room in the beauty of character,
a charm deeper than the grace of figure or
the tincture of the skin; and Raynald, when
he observed her, often quoted to himself
that saying of the wise man, "Favour is
deceitful and beauty is vain, but a woman
that feareth the Lord, she shall be praised."

CHAPTER V.

RAYNALD.

RAYNALD paused as he entered the chamber of sickness, and a smile passed over his features when he perceived Ardoine ministering to her mother. Whenever he raised that latch he felt the reverence attached to hallowed ground, for the enthusiasm of youth had thrown an atmosphere of mystery about the bedridden martyr on account of her suffering and piety.

The sight of his dying uncle and aunt lying side by side upon that bed had never been forgotten, and that first image of death had been engraven among his most lasting impressions.

Had she been imprisoned in that room
for twenty-one years? Did her captivity
begin soon after his birth? Could he con-
dense the chasing phases of boyhood and
youth, and contrast them with that mono-
tony of pain? During that time he had
received his education; he had been on a
mission to the sister churches in Switzerland and Bohemia; he had crossed the
Alps, and penetrated into France, wandering among the Montagnards of Cevennes,
and on the slopes of Leberon; he had
visited the classic cities of northern Italy,
to collate experiences and remodel the
impressions of childhood. Each time he
had bidden his aunt, as he thought, a last
adieu, but each time returned to find her
where he had left her, unchanged in place,
unchanged in feeling, awaiting her summons, triumphant through the death and
merits of her Redeemer.

When at home he read the Scriptures to
her daily, and his delicate and thoughtful

attentions did honour to his manhood, being such as are generally considered the peculiar glory of woman.

It was his delight to scale the mountain for the first gentian, so softly blue when embedded in its crystal shrine of snow, and to place it in that thin wan hand. He was jealous that Aunt Marie should taste the first fruits of the vineyard, and for her he reserved the last treasures of the orchard.

Now that he was grown up, was he additionally attracted to her bedside by the hope of meeting one who was dearer to him than life ? Was it to hear the voice of Ardoine ? To look into her sunny eyes ? To see her in an aspect so calculated to win moral homage ? Admitting that this had a share in his thoughts, let us not detract from his tried devotion to his aunt; that he unconsciously sought companionship with her he loved was but a proof that he was human, and swayed by the world-wide instincts of our common nature.

"How are you, to-day, aunt?" said Raynald, taking his seat by her bedside.

"I feel no abatement of my pains, dear nephew; but that does not ruffle my peace. I rejoice in thinking that in a moment I may be with my Saviour who is all in all to me."

"Then you are not afraid of death? My heart often trembles when I think of it, and my faith fails."

"Look to Christ," said the sufferer, "He has swallowed up death in victory. The dark valley is lighted up by his presence, and He has left me the shadow and not the substance."

"Oh! tell me," exclaimed Raynald, with earnestness, "how is it that you are able to be always the same?"

"His promises are my support. He told us on the cross that his work was finished, and this is the true ground of faith and comfort. I plead nothing but Christ and his merits. Jesus drank up the dregs of the cup of sorrow, and suffered for us from the manger to the cross."

"I find my love to Christ so cold; I can love a fellow-creature warmly, but alas, towards Him, whom I should love best, it often seems more an idea than a feeling."

"I can truly say," replied she, "that Christ is the idol of my soul. Oh! if I had ten thousand tongues, I could sound in every ear the love of Christ! He lived and died for us; his blood was shed for us; his promises are yea and amen. I love Him because He first loved me. What must the glories of heaven be!" continued the sufferer, as her whisper grew louder from animation. "I can't understand them yet, no, not till I get there, though my soul is always flooded with the assurance thereof which it would be impossible to describe."

"But is it not possible for people to deceive themselves, dear aunt?"

"You can't deceive yourself if you go to Jesus and take Him in his own way.

Satan will try to deceive you, but Jesus and Satan reflect a different light, and give a different peace."

"Tell me, what is the chief desire of your heart?"

"Holiness is all my desire; I want to be perfect in Christ. Sin is the abhorrence of my soul, and my worst cross."

"Are you never tempted to murmur?"

"Bless God, his grace prevents that. I thank Him for all his dispensations. All his chastisements breathe love into my soul."

"What is the secret of your strength?"

"I can do nothing without the Holy Spirit. Without Him I cannot think one good thought; we could not offer our hearts to God of ourselves, we must go to the cross, and conquer through the Holy Spirit."

"Oh, when shall my soul burst the chains of sin, and reach the fulness of Christ; but I will wait the Lord's leisure, as I am sealed with the blood of Jesus unto the day of redemption."

"Do you think," asked Raynald, after a pause, "that from obedience to the will of God you could go through your sufferings again?"

"I should not be dissatisfied to suffer for twenty-two years more, if it were for the glory of God; for He is quite able to support me, and Christ has promised to sit by my furnace. I was once impatient to die, but not so now, for I can leave all to Him."

Ardoine, who was seated on the foot of the bed, appeared engrossed with her knitting, but she raised her head from time to time, and cast an affectionate glance towards her mother and cousin, which was secretly observed, and often involuntarily intercepted by the latter.

"I met one of our neighbour's sons to-day, aunt, and I had some conversation with him about the sufficiency of Christ's

merits. I said how much pleasanter it is to
think that Christ's blood cleanses us at once,
than to have to make up the deficiency in
purgatory, which is an insult to Christ, as if
He had left the very work He came to do
incomplete. He listened to me attentively," continued Raynald, furtively glancing at Ardoine, to see if she was interested, "and desired to hear more on the
subject."

"Oh, I am so glad," replied Marie,
"you don't know what delight I feel when
I hear of others receiving the true faith.
It gives one unspeakable joy to hear of
conversions; I would grasp all the world
and take them to Christ; my heart is so
enlarged for the whole world."

"You are talking too much, dear aunt,
you look so pale and tired to-day," said
Raynald, pressing her hand.

"Oh, transporting thought, to think I
shall soon be in heaven! I am a sinner,
but redeemed by grace, 'free grace.' Health

would be a great drawback to me, to bring me back to this world. If I were well I might become self-sufficient and cold."

"Ardoine," said Raynald, addressing his cousin, "what a pleasure it is for us to hear your dear mother's experiences, and to have our faith confirmed by this living proof of God's power and faithfulness."

"Speak gently, Raynald," replied Ardoine, placing her finger on her lips; "mother has had a restless night, and still feels the excitement of the children's visit. She seems as if she were inclined to sleep."

There was silence in the room for some moments. Marie had dozed off into a fitful slumber. Raynald then approached his cousin, and with an expression of hope, shaded by fear, whispered in a low voice—

"Dear Ardoine, this New Year's day is a day of general happiness, will you grant me a favour as my New Year's present, especially as you know it is my birthday?"

"Certainly, dear Raynald, I may unhesitatingly confide in your prudence and discretion, and I will grant your favour before it is named."

"And you will not be angry with me ?"

"How could I be angry with one so thoughtful and affectionate as you are ? Does not your kindness to my mother endear you to a daughter's heart."

Raynald sighed and made no reply. The breathing of the sleeper was distinctly audible, and both regarded her for a moment with silent interest.

"Come, Raynald," said Ardoine, in a whisper, "name your favour, that I may have the pleasure of granting it."

"It is," said Raynald, respectfully taking Ardoine's hand and pressing it to his lips, "that you will allow me to tell you——"

"Oh, Raynald !" said Ardoine, starting to her feet, "listen to that noise in the direction of St. Jean. It has awakened mother. Oh, what do I hear ? It sounds

like the tumult of a mob in our village. There! did you hear? Is not
that the shot of an arquebus? What
are they doing? Look!" exclaimed the
girl, rushing to the window, " there is
a faint yellowish glare yonder; something
is on fire. It is just where our temple
stands. Raynald, you are bold and
strong, I need not urge you to go and
defend our friends, if there is danger.
Consult your father. Oh, hasten and pre-
vent any bloodshedding, or the destruction
of our village."

" I will go with double energy," said
Raynald, mournfully, " if you bid me go.
Do not frighten Aunt Marie, I will come
back to you soon, I trust, with more cheer-
ing news."

CHAPTER VI.

THE TEMPLE.

THE valleys of the Waldenses had, from time immemorial, been free from the errors of Rome, and for centuries had presented no external proofs of antagonistic creeds; but this was so no longer. The Catholics had for some time past raised their chapels by the side of the Vaudois temples, and made various inroads upon this primitive church.

In 1596 the first monastic corporation had been established at La Tour, since which time, to quote an old historian, "a brood of monks multiplied there, to the great detriment of the valleys." Jesuits, Capuchins, Franciscans, Observantines, and

members cf other Romish orders, were to be
seen in every market-place, and even in the
secluded mountain glen, whose recognized
tactics were to embroil the pastors, and to
lead to collisions by insults and acts of
outrage. The village of St. Jean, from
its position on the high road from Pignerol
to La Tour, was peculiarly liable to
these incursions of the holy brotherhoods,
which, in 1654, had become more frequent
and violent.

It was on the afternoon of New Year's
day that Jean Prins, accompanied by little
Bertin, was returning home from the valley
of Angrogna. In passing through the
market-place of St. Jean he was rudely
assailed by a Capuchin monk.

"Look here," cried the latter, addressing the bystanders, " here are some of those
sneaking hypocrites who are endangering
our peace, and who have hired men to
poison our holy father, the Pope of Rome.
Countrymen, help; look at that ranting

brat of Calvin, born on the Geneva dung-
hill. You Calvinist impostors, I could
break your heads with your everlasting
Bible."

"Boy, do you see this?" said Simond,
holding up a large gilt crucifix, and grasping Bertin; "down on your knees to it, or I
will shove it down your throat." So saying
he thrust it against the child's mouth, causing the blood to flow from his lips.

"Where were you before Luther?
you're nothing but the spawn of that
German, whose father was a wretched
scraper of faggots, and yet, you vermin, you
have been always gnawing at the Holy
Roman Church."

"Mary, mother of God," continued
Simond, falling on his knees, "defend thy
holy servant Innocent X., and give us grace
to crush this brood of scorpions; let thy
displeasure rest on all the apostate kings
of Europe; blast the English Roundhead,
and the Vandal Charles Gustavus; blight

the cantons of Zurich and Basle; break open those Dutch dykes; plant thorns in the dying pillow of the Elector Palatine; may he be linked with the bull-headed Henry of England. Let them be anathema. Ye wolves! ye robbers of decent men! leave us at peace; ye escaped from the bottomless pit."

"Here, brethren, keep an eye on these heretics, they are trying to bolt. Is there no one here to wipe the lad's mouth? he'll have soiled my crucifix; I must scour it in holy water. Poor boy, how he frowns at me! stop, bring them along, and we will teach them more of our faith and practice."

With these words the Capuchin, who had succeeded in gathering a crowd around him, rushed to the Waldensian temple of San Giovanni.

"There," screamed Simond, "there's that cursed bell in this tower, notwithstanding the Duke's edict, that bell, I say, which has given the ear-ache to the pious so long, and won't let us pray; I'll smash it if I can get hold of it; it would make bullets for you French soldiers," cried he, addressing some men of Grancey's regiment who had been quartered for some months in the valley.

Having flung several stones through the windows, he proceeded to batter down the door with a hammer snatched from the adjoining forge. In rushed the crowd, heated by the monk's discourse, shouting, "*Viva la Santa Fede! Viva la Santa Chiesa Romana!*"

The soldiers, Piedmontese, French, and Irish, mingled with monks and peasants, scattered themselves through the building, and began the work of destruction.

"*Gnaffe!* where's my goblet?" cried the monk, hunting about for the sacramental chalice. "Ha! I've got it, and *per Baccho* here's the cellar—a flask of the oldest for me. You *barbets* shan't get drunk here to-night;

here's my toast," he continued, pouring out the wine into the silver vessel : " Luther and Beelzebub, may they ever be united !"

"Hold on, holy father," shouted Villalmin Roche, " we are all equal here, you mustn't have it all your own way ; give me a drink."

With these words the soldier, who had been celebrating the Feast of the Circumcision in deep draughts at the village tavern, seized the vessel out of Simond's hands, thereby upsetting most of the wine. He reeled inside the rails, and seating himself astride the table, roared out—

" Boys—boys—here—he-re's—a health to—the holy Calvin "——

"Arra wisha! and if that's what yer afther, I'll knock you clane off your perch like a blind jackdaw," said a wild-looking Irishman, snatching up a Bible and hurling it at Villalmin. The leaves whirred as the book flew through the air, and the missile struck the cup, the contents of which streamed into the soldier's bell-shaped boot.

" What's that you're after—a health to our holy father ? I say long life and a good wife for Innocent. I wish him safe into purgatory. The Pope, boys, the Pope; down and cross yourselves, or I'll baptize you with the scrapings."

" Here's the bell," interrupted Simond, with a voice of thunder; "take that," said he, hurling it with all his force against the pavement. " I think it will hold its clapper now, as our good duke ordered it to do some time ago. Children, you can worship now without hearing Belial tolling."

Meanwhile the work of destruction did not flag. The pews were torn up, the benches were flung into the aisle, the communion table and rails were piled in a heap, the registrations, the minister's robes, the Bibles and psalm-books, were rent in pieces and thrown among the *débris*. The church was filled with a clamorous crowd,

French, Irish, Piedmontese soldiers, jostling against monks, and priests, in one mass of confusion; whilst the shouts and curses of rage and fanaticism ascended to heaven from this late temple of peace like the howl of hell. The monk Simond ascended the pulpit, where for some moments he stood looking upon the havoc with a smile of malicious joy. In his left hand he carried a burning torch, and in his right a drawn sword, whilst from his waist hung a large crucifix. Making the sign of the cross with the sword, he cried out in a loud voice, "*Gloria in cœlis altissimis Deo, et in terrâ pax, in homines benevolentia.*"

The light of the pine torch glared fitfully above the crowd, and the sparks which fell from it soon kindled some of the scattered books that were lying around the pulpit.

Above the din was heard the stentorian voice of the preacher—"Thus saith the Lord, let the Church gain the victory.

By what means ? By these means," continued he, as the sword in his right hand
clanked upon the pulpit. "We must
cast out the idolater, root and branch,
with fire and sword. Use your axes and
hammers, and fulfil the words of Scripture, spoken by David the prophet—
'*Quasi in sylva lignorum securibus exciderunt
januas ejus in idipsum ; in securi et ascia
dejecerunt eam.*' I hate this brood of
heretics, who are always boasting that they
descend from the Apostles, and who talk
as if the Pope was wrong, and they were
right."

"By whom," said Simond, waxing
warm, "have I been sent here ? By the
holy council—*De propagandâ fide, et extirpandis hœreticis*—that's the last glorious
addition to their title since the jubilee of
1650; that's my motto, pluck up the beggars, raze their houses, pluck, pluck them
up, root and branch; don't stand gaping at
heresy, whilst the *barbets* are giving long-

winded references to their perverted Bible.
Saul and the Amalekites — that's the
Church's example—I'd exterminate them to
a man.   Would they had one neck, give me
the sword above it, and I'll warrant I'll not
strike twice.   If the Archbishop of Turin
and the Marquis of Pianesse don't find me
up to my work it's not my fault.   What's the
use of wasting time, spending money,
doling out bread, when there's a shorter
cut ?   ' Down with them !   down with
them ! bring them to the dust,' as say the
ancient Fathers, and the Lord of Hosts."

"Ah ! methinks I see my good friend
Malvicino amongst you, the Abbot of Pignerol, Confessor to the Marchioness of
Pianesse.   Brother, hast thou any of thy
lambs here ? any of those whose swords are
in the Church's pay ?   If so, bid them
spoil the Philistines, for their goods are
confiscated."

These words were addressed to one
whose appearance was anything but pre-

possessing. He was short in stature, and somewhat corpulent, while his eyes, dim with sensuality, betrayed rather the revels of the refectory than the vigils of the oratory.

"Holy Abbot, help us with our two converts," exclaimed Simond: "here is a boy who would do for your godly institution at Pignerol, where you educate the children of the apostates in the true faith. But it's more good luck than he deserves. Will you baptize him, Abbot?"

"By Pope Innocent VIII., and his eight sons and eight daughters, I will," exclaimed Malvicino. "Here, you young urchin, let me get hold of you."

Terrified by his looks, Bertin made a convulsive spring, and succeeded in extricating himself from the man who held him prisoner.

With breathless haste the boy ran in the direction of La Baudènc, followed by the Abbot at his utmost speed.

"Confound the wire-worm," groaned

Malvicino. "By Pope . . . who . . if I break . . my lungs . . that thin-nosed monk will get into my Abbot's chair . . which he has been so long coveting."

The Abbot had hardly disappeared before a young man of commanding height ran breathlessly into the temple.

Recovering from the momentary recoil which he experienced on beholding the scene, he rushed regardless of danger into the midst of the crowd to the place where Jean was guarded. Grasping a soldier with either hand, he dashed them backwards on the pavement.

"Quick, uncle," exclaimed Raynald. "Keep close to me. These cowards will give me a path you see."

"Ah, Ardoine," muttered the young man between his teeth, as he looked up at Simond in the pulpit, "I feel as if I could hurl that intruder from yon sacred place, where we have listened to our grandfather's voice. But for thy sake I will abstain from

ROME'S APOSTLE.

Page 77.

what might lead to bloodshed, single-handed as I am against such odds."

As he was making for the door, a fragment of wood struck him in the face, causing the blood to stream from his cheek. Regardless of his wound, he extricated himself and uncle from the crowd, considering it most prudent to return to La Baudène.

Simond, who had beheld with fear the daring exploit of Raynald, was filled with revengeful fury when he saw him depart.

"Children," said he, after recovering his breath, "it's New Year's Day, let us have an *auto da fé*. Let truth be sounded in this pulpit for the last time; let not the squinting *barbet* ruin your brethren's souls any longer. Destroy this temple, saith the Lord. *Destruite templum hoc*, and then you will be able to worship according to your conscience."

Simond now descended from the pulpit and mingled with the crowd, who needed little exhortation to glut the vengeance of bigotry and rage.

The pulpit was thrown into the centre aisle, and the crash of ruin resounded through the building. The monks gathering fragments of wood and books into a large pile, lighted them in the church.

"Marcy on us, here's a blaze," cried O'Donoghue. "The Clargy want to warm their feet, and it's right on the first of January when the frost is nipping our toes. I'll bet his riverince would like to clap that Sassenach on the top, and I should like to be afther roastin' some pratees. But I must lind a hand. God an' the blissed mother and the thrue Church for iver."

The smouldering fire soon blazed more fiercely as the pews and pulpit-rails and books were heaped one upon another.

"Here," said Simond, flinging a Bible into the pyre, "this is the heretic's text-book. Take care, touch it not, Gaspardo, or you will need a Bishop's absolution; and if you were to die suddenly, your soul might be lost for ever."

Some hewed down the doors with pick-axes, while others inserted powder into the chinks of the masonry to blast the brick-work. The walls were soon blackened. The text of Scripture over the arch, " This is life eternal, to know thee the only true God and Jesus Christ, whom thou hast sent," was no longer legible.

The leaping jets of fire scathed the rafters; they cracked and hissed, they charred and glowed, and then snapping in twain, fell into the lower ruin, bringing with them a portion of the roof. The wind now fanned the flames. The wavering lines of light struggled with the breeze, and gra-dually the columns of fire pierced the dark shadows of eve.

The fire rages, for there is no effort made to quench the devouring element. The maddened crowd dance round, singing anthems to the Virgin, and beseech her to accept this labour of love upon the first day of the New Year.

CHAPTER VII.

MALVICINO, although unable to overtake Bertin, observed him enter the avenue which led to La Baudène.

With frantic speed the child rushed into the court-yard, and his screams soon brought Ardoine to his assistance. Malvicino, who seemed determined not to lose his prize, eagerly followed him through the archway. On entering the yard, the Abbot seemed suddenly struck with astonishment, and looked round upon the building as if to assure himself of the actual locality.

" Two-and-twenty years," muttered he to himself. " Can it be the same place ?

By Pope Alexander's poisoned cups, if that wine has not clouded my brain it is the very same. How time rolls on! Are they the same people? There seems to be a family likeness. Ha! Ha! they should thank me, if they remember me, for the good service I once rendered them."

"Ha!" said he, raising his head, and perceiving Ardoine, "what have we here? A good-looking girl; that anchorite Borgia would have admired her profile! If I could get hold of her I would resign the lad, and let him and the rest of them go to the devil their own way."

He then approached Ardoine, who was so occupied at the fountain, in washing away the stain of blood from Bertin's mouth, that she was unaware of his presence. She looked up on hearing his footstep, and grew pale with speechless terror when she found herself thus suddenly confronted with a Romish ecclesiastic.

"Do not fear, my daughter," said the

Abbot, addressing Ardoine in his smoothest tone. "The lad has been baptized; he is our property, but I will resign him for your sake, if you will——"

"Hold!" said Raynald, in a voice of thunder, as he entered the court, and having heard the Abbot's speech, perceived the danger in which Ardoine and the child were placed—

"Touch not the lad, profane kidnapper, or your monkish cowl shall not save you from a brother's vengeance."

Malvicino was hesitating as to what line of conduct he should adopt, when the unexpected entrance of two of the ruffians in the pay of his abbey, who had followed him in the distance, offered the solution of his difficulty.

"Soldiers," said the Abbot, "you have come at the right time. Yon lad is the property of our convent, and it is our duty to save his soul. By Pope Hildebrand do your work boldly, as we pay you well.

Methinks the two of you are a match for that fellow even if he were inclined to resist, which I hope, for his own sake, he is not."

The two men advanced in order to seize Bertin,—but they had misjudged their antagonist. Springing forward, Raynald grasped the foremost round his waist, and threw him into the water which surrounded the fountain. One blow was sufficient to disable the second, whose sword fell from his powerless grasp.

Malvicino did not wait to see more, but retreated at his utmost speed.

"Some other time," he gasped, "I will see her again. . . After so long a time I had forgotten the place. But one . . must be cautious with such people. Profane kidnapper! . . What did he mean? Does he hint at——? No. . . By Pope . . who . . an idea strikes me. . . It comes from the Virgin; I will say four more *Aves* . . to-night in her honour . . if I can get safely back to Pignerol."

"Oh, stop!" exclaimed Ardoine, as Raynald bent over the fallen soldier; "do not kill them. We must return good for evil. I think Bertin is more frightened than hurt."

"If they had touched you I could not have forgiven them; but since you intercede for them I will do nothing more."

"Oh, Raynald!" exclaimed Ardoine, as a gleam of light fell on his face, "what's the matter with you? you are hurt. I see blood on your cheek. Oh forgive me if I did not think of you, I, who sent you into the danger."

The tone of unfeigned agitation in which these words were uttered caused a glow of pleasure to light up Raynald's countenance. He listened to those expressions of interest with breathless eagerness, and his voice trembled as he replied—

"I am not much hurt, it's only a flesh wound, though it has bled a great deal. I

will wash it first, and then go to Aunt
Lucille for some of her stores; she is
always praising the virtues of her *calendula*,
and I will give her the opportunity of heal-
ing me quickly."

"Dear Raynald, let me help you; here
is my handkerchief, let me dip it in the
water, and that may refresh you."

"What will you think of me, dear
Ardoine, if this wound should leave a scar?
shall you not be afraid to look at me?"

"Afraid to look at you, dear Raynald!
no, that scar would only serve to remind
me of your bravery, and that there is no
one else in our valley so self-forgetful as
you are."

"Then I trust I shall have the scar,"
replied the mountaineer, with a smile. "If
you think thus, I shall be well rewarded.
But here is my mother coming. I must
hasten and wash away these marks, or she
will be alarmed. I see lights, so I suppose
it is time to assemble, and I hear Etienne

calling me.   Go to them, Ardoine, but do
not frighten them, for they cannot know
anything of what has just happened."

"Where is Raynald?" said Lucille, addressing Ardoine as she entered the room.
"It must be something unusual which
makes him late this New Year's evening,
and he is usually so punctual in taking
Marie her *potage* every night."

"I thought," said Etienne, "that I
saw him a little while ago behind those
chesnuts. His food will be cold, and we
shall have finished before he begins."

"Oh! what is the matter?" exclaimed
Martha, as her son entered. "Look at
Raynald's face. Has anything happened?"

"Speak! has anything happened to
any of the children?" exclaimed Madeleine.

.   "No, not that," replied Raynald, with
emotion. "Our temple has been destroyed.
It is burning now; its very stones are
broken, it is one mass of wreck and ruin,"
continued he, bursting into tears.

The whole family were prostrated by this sudden blow, and nothing but sighs and lamentations could be heard in the room.

"Children, children!" said Rodolphe, "look up to heaven, and weep not. God dwells not in temples made with hands, nor is his presence confined to walls or rooms. He is near us here. Let us feel his presence, and his peace will outweigh our trials. 'In everything give thanks,' says the apostle, and this includes adversity as well as prosperity. 'There be many that say, Who will show us any good? Lord, lift thou up the light of thy countenance upon us.'"

"But," said Etienne, sobbing bitterly, "shall we have no temple to go to on Sunday? What will Barba Léger do if his pulpit is gone? Oh, how cruel it must be of them to take away our churches! How wicked of the Duke; I would tell him so if I could speak to him."

"No, my child, the Duke has not done

it, and perhaps knows nothing of it. It is the act of a few persons, I should think, who have been urged on by the missionary monks, who are always trying to embroil us."

"But they have their own churches," continued the boy, whose feelings were not to be quieted with calm reasonings. "There is a church opposite ours. When I passed once, I heard a bell, and I peeped in, and saw lighted candles, and men bowing in all sorts of strange ways. Will they have their churches, and shan't we have ours?"

"Alas, they will. Some years ago there were no other churches here but our own, but the council of Turin has established convents everywhere; and now, on this blessed soil, which has been so long free and unpolluted, Rome has got places of worship, to teach error and promote discord."

"Oh, it's very strange," said the boy,

brushing away his falling tears, "they seem such different people to what we read of in the Bible. Do you think, grandfather, that good man, Daniel, would have done the same things?"

"No, I do not; all force is contrary to a religion which demands the heart, and comes from a God of love. We must never act like wicked men in order to bring people to Christ; the wrath of man can never work the righteousness of God."

"Then all these men, with their dark faces, and long brown dresses, what are they—are they the monks?"

"Yes, missionary monks, sent to preach and to intermeddle in everything possible, so as to produce distrust, and prejudice the Duke against us."

"Perhaps they have burnt our temple; and I am sure they ought not, for ours was so very plain. I saw all sorts of pictures and statues in theirs; why have not we the same?"

" Because the second commandment
forbids it."

" But doesn't it forbid them as
well !"

" It does, but they leave it out."

" Then they haven't ten commandments," said the boy, who in the sweet
fickleness of childhood had, for the moment,
forgotten his grief.

" To make up ten, they divide the tenth
into two; and in the same way they don't
mind the fourth, which tells us to keep the
Sabbath holy, but they say, ' Keep the fes-
tivals holy.' You know we cannot work
when it is a saint's day in the Romish
Calendar, and this makes us lose a great
many days."

" We seem to like work better than they
do," said Etienne, " for whilst we are in
the fields we see many of them running
about in fine dresses, and when they come
to a cross, or a picture with a light before
it on the road side, they kneel down and

cross themselves. Did God tell them to
do this?"

"No, my child, but fetch me my Bible;
stop, never mind, there's dear Ardoine
bringing it."

"Children," said Rodolphe, addressing
his sons and daughters, who were bewailing
their loss among themselves, "let us conclude
the day which began brightly, but whose
close a cloud has darkened; let us conclude
it with the Word of God and prayer.
The events of this evening are a sad comment on the words I spake to you this
morning. My heart is full and heavy. In
that pulpit, my daughters, I preached well
nigh threescore years ago. When I was
the only pastor of our valley who survived
the plague I did not desert that church, and
it is now a ruin, and yonder sky is coloured
by its glowing embers."

"Ah, Paul, thou wast right to remind
us that we are but strangers here, for they
have destroyed even the houses of God in

the land.   Let us once more, my children,
betake ourselves to Him who is a hiding-
place from the storm, who can cover us
with his feathers, and keep us safe in his
secret habitation."

Rodolphe then read in a trembling
voice the following verses, which touched
the hearts of all the afflicted worshippers :—

" God is our refuge and strength, a
very present help in trouble.   Therefore
will not we fear, though the earth be
removed, and though the mountains be
carried into the midst of the sea ; though
the waters thereof roar and be troubled,
though the mountains shake with the swel-
ling thereof.   Selah.   *   *   *   *   *
Come, behold the works of the Lord, what
desolations he hath made in the earth.
He maketh wars to cease unto the end of
the earth ; he breaketh the bow, and
cutteth the spear in sunder ; he burneth
the chariot in the fire.   Be still, and know

that I am God: I will be exalted among the heathen, I will be exalted in the earth. The Lord of hosts is with us; the God of Jacob is our refuge. Selah." (Psalm xlvi. 1—3; 8—11.)

The old man then gave his family his patriarchal blessing, and retired to rest.

CHAPTER VIII.

THE FEMALE PROPAGANDA.

In an ancient palace overlooking the Piazza
Castello at Turin, a small party of ladies
were assembled. Their fashionable dress
and noble mien indicated that they were
persons of rank. It was evident from their
serious countenances, and the pens, ink, and
paper which lay on the table round which
they were seated, that they had not met for
the purpose of amusement, but to transact important business. One to whom the others paid
marked deference presided. Her dress, of the
richest quality, was profusely ornamented,
and contrasted strangely with her haggard
eye, the symptom of disease and care.

"My ladies," said she, "we have met to give in our weekly report, and to see what progress the cause of the Holy Faith makes in our hands. Let us not flag in zeal, but show the world what women can do for the suppression of heresy, for we form the female branch of the *Congregatio de propagandâ Fide, et extirpandis Hœreticis.*"

"Let us hear first," said the Marchioness of Angrogna, "what the noble President herself has done."

"My strength is not equal to my will," replied the Marchioness of Pianesse, "for I have felt the attacks of an old complaint, which has often threatened my life. Still I have endeavoured to carry out the decisions of the Council, as agreed at our previous meetings."

. "I thought," said the Countess of Lucerna, "I saw your Grace bent on some labour of love last week in the Borgo Dora, with your purse in your hand."

"Ladies," continued the President, who spake with some difficulty, "you remember that we divided Turin and its neighbourhood into districts, and arranged that each should visit their district twice a-week to collect the alms of the faithful. Owing to my illness I have not been at my post more than once this week. I have, however, canvassed all those low cabarets which lie near the river Dora, and I must confess that I was surprised at my favourable reception. I went boldly into the taverns, and, holding out my purse, demanded a piece of money for the maintenance of the faith, and the suppression of heresy."

"I wonder at your moral courage, Marchioness," replied a lady at the further end of the table, "I feel as if I dare not venture into those dens."

"Remember for whom you are working. The Virgin will protect you and reward you hereafter. Where did you go, Duchess?"

"I went into the gambling-houses overlooking the Po, and asked alms from the maddened players for the conversion of souls. I think some of them knew me, having seen me at Court, for they were civil enough, and one swore he hoped we should destroy that brood of heretics in the adjoining valleys."

"The Virgin grant it!" said the Marchioness. "It is of little moment to win over individuals when there is that reservoir of heresy in those mountains. I must speak to the Marquis, and see if the secular arm will not aid us; I think the government would give us an edict or two to serve our purpose."

"I feel sure it would," replied the Duchess of Montafon, "for Madame Royale has her heart in this matter, and she can mould the Duke. I think we' should stir them up to enforce the edict of Gastaldo of the 15th of May, 1650, and try its effect."

"We must leave the political part of

it to our husbands, and the council of state; besides, our branch council, under the guidance of the Archbishop and the Marquis, will not forget this."

"Don't you think, Marchioness," said the Countess of Bagnol, "that we ought to supply the missionary monks in the valleys with more means of charity? There has been a great deal of famine there, and when the heretics are starving we have fine scope for conversions — starving people cannot resist bread, and they would accept it upon the terms of going to mass."

"I think the idea is good, but we have tried it, and I confess with very little success. Two years ago the convents were stocked with every article needed, and relief given only to those who would swear to go to mass, but the *ruse* succeeded with a mere handful."

"The obstinacy of these heretics is amazing," said the Countess of Lucerna, with a sigh; "they lose their property, their homes, their lives, and all is offered to them again, with every privilege, if they will but reform, and yet they will not."

"It shows it must be the work of the devil," said the Marchioness, "for it appears as if our Holy Father himself had no power to exorcise them."

"Where have you been, Countess?"

"I have been through the prisons, collecting alms for the general fund, testing the prisoners, and promising release to any of the pretended reformed faith who would become Catholics; but, to be candid, I doubt whether I found three or four Protestants among the number."

"I tell you what I will suggest to the Marquis," said the president; "if he has to execute the Church's vengeance, and the secular arm is used, he would find many valuable allies in the prisons, and we should have no difficulty in opening the prison doors."

"No; a plenary indulgence is promised to all who engage in this holy work,
and assuredly many of these poor fellows
need it! After all, their crimes, horrible
as they are, are not so execrable as that of
heresy."

"There is one convert I hope to
win," said the lady president; "he is a
young man from the valleys in France; he
was engaged in speculations, and is under
arrest; I could see by the despair on his
countenance, when he thought of his wife
and children, that he is on the brink of
ruin. We have him regularly in our power,
and I offered to free him from all legal
proceedings if he would become a Catholic.
He seemed to waver when I reminded him
of the misery which was hanging over his
family, and how easily he might be restored
to comfort."

"I have been thinking over your plan,
Marchioness," said the Countess of Bagnol,
"about sending some of our agents as

servants among the Vaudois. I think it offers many advantages. The servant would be able, in a hundred little ways, to instil our principles into the minds of the children, to prejudice them against their creed, and besides we could take advantage of any divisions in the family; she could set the daughter against her mother, and the mother against the daughter; and, surely, if we could sow some family dissensions, the Church might reap her harvest."

"The suggestion is excellent, and worthy of a trial, and I will make the experiment in a family in the Valley of Lucerna, of which my confessor, the Abbot of Pignerol, has been telling me. It is a peculiar family, for six brothers have married six sisters, and they live together without division of property, and without discord, numbering, with their children, upwards of forty persons."

"That would be a glorious field; there must, surely, be some among that number not so obstinate; at any rate, we could not have better scope for the trial of this holy artifice."

" I hate those Pharisees, I think they're called, who affect to be over-righteous," said the Countess of Lucerna, drawing herself up with stately pomp. " Their conduct and manner of talking seem to be a perpetual reproach to our Holy Church, and I highly approve of the last suggestion."

" Do you know of any one who would suit ?" asked the Marchioness of Angrogna, speaking in a low tone to her next neighbour.

"There is a woman," replied the Duchess of Montafon, "in the dungeons of the castle, who would answer; she is under sentence of death for the murder of her husband, who detected her shortcomings; but I can liberate her if I speak to the Duke, and tell him she is wanted for the service of the Holy Church. She is a clever woman, and withal of bland and winning manners. She appears to be the very instrument."

"But would she be ready to accept the terms? Perhaps her conscience might object."

"Conscience object! Why, Marchioness, you are talking nonsense. If your conscience and mine do not object, I think the conscience of a murderess need not be so scrupulous. Besides, it's for the Church, and you know what our confessor told us was Cardinal Bellarmine's dictum, 'that the end justifies the means.'"

"You silence me with your quotation. You know I am no theologian, and leave the schools to the priests. I want to work out my salvation, and if my reverend father approves, I will join heart and hand in any good work for the benefit of others."

"I think I have a friend," said the Marchioness of Pianesse aloud, "who will accept the office for the good of her soul,

and the glory of the Church. I will per-
suade her to undertake the matter."

"You know," continued she, speaking
aside in a lower tone to her neighbour,
"we ought to be diligent in the Church's
service. Remember a plenary indulgence
is promised to all engaged in the holy work
of suppressing heresy; and I think, between you and me, that there are several
of us who need this plenary absolution, at
least I confess I do. I know I have much
to answer for when I look at the past,
and my only hope is, that during the
short time I have to live, my zeal may
atone for the faults of my early life. If
I could help to cleanse Italy from the
blot of heresy, my conscience would have
more peace."

"You are severe upon yourself," interposed the Countess; "we need not allude
to the past; whatever we have been, and
we all know the laxity of the times, we
received absolution from the moment

that we became members of this holy council."

"Ladies," continued the Marchioness, in a languid voice, "I think the dispersion of the missionary monks through the valley, and the cantonment of troops, will produce good fruit. The establishment of a Monte di Pieta is excellent. In this time of distress the loan of wheat, and provisions, and garments has been a real boon. If any one accepts anything it is easy to press more on them, and when they are deeply in our debt we threaten ruin or the mass."

"Capital," exclaimed all the ladies together, "your invention, Marchioness, on behalf of the Church, is happily consecrated to the noblest object."

"If," continued the Marchioness, "they will come over to the true Church, then we remit all their past debts, give them a large sum, and free them from all taxes, imposts, and exactions, for the space of

five years, with an increased time, if they
show themselves zealous in the cause."

"Have you seen any fruit from the
family spy to whom you were alluding?"
asked one of the younger ladies.

"I think so; she has artfully embroiled
a young married couple of the pretended
reformed faith, and they are going to law
with each other; so we shall be able to
ruin them, or to turn the verdict in favour
of the one who will abjure."

"You said, Marchioness, you have a
friend who would go into a Vaudois family.
How can you introduce her among them?"

"Oh, that is easily done; for we need
not say who she is. You know they have
soldiers there, and we can either billet her
on a family, or send her with a medical
certificate for change of air, or get the
Duke to write an order requesting them to
lodge her, as a proof of loyalty."

"Ha, ha! commend me to the Marchioness of Pianesse for ways and means."

" Oh ! but here is a better idea—she can represent herself as an inquirer, as one who was a Catholic, but has met with a Vaudois at Turin, and wants more instruction in the reformed faith. This will be a regular appeal to their prejudices, and will be done gently, without disturbance."

" What a field she will have ! What do you say ? Six brothers married to six sisters. Why, really, it's a lovely pastoral, worthy of an eclogue ; it is almost a pity to mar such a scene, which would elicit one of Petrarch's sonnets. Would they were Catholics ! but they are heretics, and as such are doomed to everlasting ruin by the Vicar of Christ and the General Councils. Nought but blood can bring relief, I suppose, nor blot out the stain. We must, however, labour for their salvation ; and may the Virgin grant us good success !"

After the discussion of some minor details, the council of missionary ladies separated.

" Oh, my soul, come not thou in their secret; unto their assembly, mine honour be not thou united; for their words are softer than oil, yet be they drawn swords."

CHAPTER IX.

THE MARCHIONESS.

THE Marchioness of Pianesse, after another consultation with her confessor, Malvicino, did not delay bringing the proposition before her niece, Iolande, whom she considered suitable for the purpose, and over whom she had always exercised considerable influence.

"The council of ladies belonging to the Propaganda," said the Marchioness, addressing her niece, "has lately met, and we all feel the necessity of increased devotion to our holy work, to efface from our land the stain of heresy. A plan was discussed at our last meeting, in which I think you can help us; you will, I am sure, be glad to labour for the glory of God, and the good of your own soul."

"I shall feel it a privilege, aunt, to assist your efforts for the holy cause by any means that lie within my humble power."

"I have spoken to my confessor, Malvicino, who suggested the plan. We propose that you should enter a Waldensian family, in order to convert some of them. I know it may be a trial to your feelings to live in a farm, but it will be only for a short time, and you will not mind a little self-sacrifice for the good of the Church. Our history is full of noble precedents of self-renunciation. So go in among them, sow suspicions and jealousies, fan every element of discord. Mould the minds of the young children, and familiarize them with the names of the Catholic saints, and your efforts, under the Virgin's blessing, I doubt not will bring forth good fruit."

"But I am afraid, aunt, I am hardly

suited to such a task. It would require a great deal of tact, and knowledge of character. Your proposal indeed takes me so much by surprise that you must excuse my hesitation."

"I hope it is not the fear of self-sacrifice that keeps you back; nothing great or good can be done without self-forgetful zeal."

"I trust that is not my motive; but the idea is so new to me, that I shrink within myself at the contemplation of its difficulties."

"You must pray to the Mother of God for help, and I am sure it will be granted."

"Well, but aunt, the first point is to know where I am to go. Have you any particular place in your mind?"

"I think so. I have heard of a most peculiar family, offering us a fine field for conversions. It is composed of six brothers married to six sisters, living together in Arcadian style, numbering with their children over forty persons."

"But I'm afraid they will be suspicious, and not receive me," replied Iolande.

"You must profess to be dissatisfied with the Catholic religion, and having met a Vaudois traveller at Turin, you want to hear more about their creed,—and once in, you know what we do at Court ; you can entangle some young man, I think, can't you?"

"No, no, aunt, I am not so skilled in playing fast and loose with the young men," replied the girl, blushing, fearing lest her attachment to the son of the Marchioness might be discovered.

"Again, you know there are many bands of robbers about, and your father's estates are not far from Cavour, you can act as our ancestors did nearly a hundred years ago, in the time of the Count de la Trinité, and take refuge among them to preserve your honour."

"Did they do this in the last century ? I wonder our people were not afraid to trust themselves among the heretics."

"No fear of that; they treated them like sisters, there was not one of them insulted; we could not trust them in La Tour, although it was full of the Catholic soldiers of the cross."

"That's strange, aunt, and if we are to judge of them by their fruits, it seems to speak rather well for the practical effect of heresy."

"Hush! don't speak in that way. Our confessor would say that smells of heresy. The infallible Church stoops not to argue nor inquire. We demand implicit faith, and then all is well."

"I have been brought up in the Church," said Iolande, "but I don't much like this commission; my conscience does not approve of deliberately sowing discord among such brethren. This cannot surely be right."

"It's for their souls' good, my dear, as well as for ours; the Bible, my confessor told me, says that the mother shall be set against her daughter, and the daughter-in-law against her mother-in-law, and that Christ came to make a man's foes those of his own household; so you need not fear, for you will go with the authority of the Church."

"I don't much like it, aunt, my natural feelings are against it."

"A plenary indulgence is promised to all who engage in the work, and admitting that we stretch a moral point in what we do, a dispensation from Rome will make all right. Consider how long those people have been a thorn in our eyes. Pope after Pope has endeavoured to uproot them, yet they still cling to their rocks. They send out their proselytisers everywhere. They boast of greater antiquity than we do. They say that their doctrine has come down in an unbroken chain from the apostles themselves, and that they hold the primitive truth uncorrupt, that they differ from the reformed churches in Ger-

many, because they have never been reformed. Think of these insults. They
quote their eternal Bible to prove that we
are Antichrist, and even on the rack and
in death they hold fast their doctrines with
the most pertinacious obstinacy. Oh think,
will you not help, if you can do anything
in the holy cause, anything to wipe away
our reproach?"

"Your statements, aunt, are urgent,
and if so weak an instrument as I can sub-
serve the cause of truth, I feel that my
duty is to obey."

"It is, to obey those who have the
spiritual rule over you. Besides, consider
the effect on your own soul. Such a work
as this makes your own salvation more
certain, and if you feel any repugnance to
the work, there is greater merit in over-
coming your natural aversion, and sacri-
ficing your conscience and the dictates of
your private judgment for the sake of the
welfare of the Holy Catholic and Apostolic

Church. Remember our principles—the end justifies the means, faith is not to be kept with heretics, and that good is your object. Besides, a dispensation will make all right, for Bellarmine says, that a sin would cease to be a sin if the Pope so decrees it. Go, therefore, niece, to your work of faith and labour of love."

"If the Church commands me," said Iolande, "I will do what I can in that family, and I hope the blessed Virgin will look favourably on my weak efforts, and enable me to follow your zeal for the propagation of the faith and the extirpation of heresy."

"May the Virgin grant it, my beloved Iolande," said the Marchioness, kissing her on the forehead.

CHAPTER X.

IOLANDE.

IOLANDE found no difficulty in introducing herself to the hospitable circle at La Baudène, whose loyalty and religious feelings inclined them to attach credit to her statement, without scrutinizing her motives. She was kindly received by all the inmates, and by her bland and studied manners soon won her way into the family, more credulous because themselves incapable of hypocrisy or guile. As she conjectured that her success would be greatest among the young, she took every means of ingratiating herself with Ardoine. From her she learned the various details about the family, their characters, and personal peculiarities.

Having been brought up at Turin, she had acquired what is called knowledge of the world, and the art of dissembling, but she found it difficult perpetually to wear the mask before Ardoine, whose artless sincerity and transparency of motive often marred her best-concerted plans.

She attentively studied Raynald's disposition. His simplicity of character, his impulsive temper, his religious yearnings formed a phase of human nature which she had not observed elsewhere. With woman's insight she speedily discerned the secret of his heart; and though she loved another, and cared not to win him for herself, she nevertheless determined to avail herself of this knowledge as affording material for future intrigue.

The farm of La Baudène offered a wide scope for the machinations of Rome. A family so large and united was a rare moral spectacle; enough for Rome's anger to know that its members were heretics. To them, according to the Papal exposition, chap. xiii. 1 Corinthians had no application. The Church would be more glorified in marring this moral loveliness than in producing like fruits in her own circle. But, thanks to the goodness and affection of the sisters, Iolande's casual insinuations produced no injurious effect. She was therefore more assiduous to impress the younger members of the family. When she walked with the children she would narrate legends and miracles of the Romish saints, and with the proverbial zeal of Jesuitism neglected no opportunity of artfully tampering with the principles or tempers of her young disciples. After patient manœuvres, she succeeded in fomenting a quarrel between Bertin and Valère, which was a source of sorrow to all, and, from its rare occurrence, was more keenly felt by the parents; but she carried out her plans with such secrecy and tact that the household did not suspect the character of their guest. Unremitting in her

attentions to Rodolphe, she would even read
to him his portions of Scripture, and not
being naturally of an evil disposition, many
of the passages fell upon her heart with
their native force, and caused her conscience
to tremble with self-accusation. She had,
however, gone too far to recede. She was
compromised with Malvicino, and when her
moral sense rebelled against the use of un-
holy artifices for the interests of the Church,
she stifled her misgivings by the assurance
that she was labouring for the Virgin and
for the promotion of her own salvation. It
is written, " Yea, the time cometh that who-
soever killeth you will think that he doeth
God service."

She communicated regularly with Malvicino and the Marchioness, who exhorted
her by every motive to carry on the holy
work of promoting discord among heretics.

There was another feeling which ere
long touched her woman's heart, and which
more than her religious feeling urged the

accomplishment of her mission. It was
jealousy of Ardoine. She could not look
upon that sunny brow and cloudless eye
without a pang of envy, and yet the rank-
ling feeling was excited not so much by
Ardoine's beauty as by that nameless grace,
that winning artlessness, that simplicity
of manner, which invested her as with a
moral halo, and shone in her most trifling
act or speech. In beauty Ardoine was,
perhaps, hardly her rival, but in moral
character she was vastly her superior. This
Iolande involuntarily acknowledged, when
she contrasted her wilful designs with the
guileless freedom of the mountain girl.

Raynald, notwithstanding his impulsive-
ness, was not destitute of observation of
character, and from the first had looked
upon her with no special favour. Iolande
soon perceived this, and was, therefore,
more assiduous in plying him with artful
questions about different points of faith,
and in asking for refutations of the Romish

errors.   She listened attentively, and spoke
in a way to captivate the vanity of the
young man, who would have been more than
human had he disdained the incense.   She
was, however, drifting to a result different
from her coldly-matured plans.   In spite of
herself, and notwithstanding a previous attachment, she became insensibly interested
in Raynald.   The rough sincerity of his
character, his inaccessibility, his disregard of
those arts with which men approach women,
this made his conquest more piquant—to
one who had lived in the gaiety of cities,
and had been the sought and not the
seeker.   But more than all, she enjoyed the
prospective triumph of robbing Ardoine of
her lover, which would be a gratification to
her womanly vanity, and a stroke of policy
on behalf of the Holy Church.

" Pullies had been fixed in the beams of the ceiling, from which descended several ropes, supporting in the air an antique couch."

Page 123.

CHAPTER XI.

THE DEATH-BED.

OUR scene is laid once more in the spacious tapestried apartment where the female Propaganda had met a few weeks before. The arrangements of the room had been altered in the most extraordinary manner. Pullies had been fixed in the great transverse beams of the ceiling, from which descended several ropes, supporting in the air an antique couch, richly decorated and surmounted by a gilded coronet. In this strange aerial bed lay a woman, not much past middle age, but now struggling with death. A restless and fierce expression shone in her eyes, which glowed in her hollow cheeks, wan from suffering and want of sleep.   After an interval of silence a paroxysm of misery darkened her countenance.

"Oh, the fire, the fire," she screamed, "save me from the flames; they surround me on every side."

"Lift up my bed, pull it up higher; it's on fire, it's on fire.   I feel the grasp of the flame.   Can you not hear me, you accursed minx?" said she, addressing her nurse. "Pull the ropes, hoist me up higher—to the ceiling—higher."

"Alas !" sobbed the aged woman in a corner of the room, "to think that my darling mistress, whom I was the first to nurse, should have come to this."

"Do you hear?" screamed the sufferer. "I tell you the flames are underneath my bed; why don't you help me? Hoist up the bed. You don't lift me out, nor bring me water. I feel the fire. A curse on your withered cheeks. Holy Madonna, water, water from heaven."

"Take off those rats," continued the apparent maniac, after a pause; "I feel them gnawing me. Oh, they are running over me."

"Take them off. Oh, how I suffer! Was it in this room that I sat as the president of that blessed Council for the extirpation of heresy? I am dying; I am dying; and the bitterness of the flame adds to the pangs of unwelcome death."

The servant, anxious to soothe the frantic paroxysm of her mistress, tightened the ropes, and raised the bed six or eight feet from the ground, until its canopy touched the ceiling. As she was fastening the cord a side door opened, and four persons entered. One, who was the husband of the sufferer, approached the bed, and beckoned to the attendant to lower it to the floor. He was dressed in the uniform of a general. His demeanour was soft, but yet

the subtle cunning in that eye pronounced
his manners to be the schooled hypocrisy of
Jesuitism. His companion was an officer
in the army, in the prime of life. His dark
eyes flashed from under his high forehead
with an ingenuous daring arguing nobility
of soul. The third was an ecclesiastic of
high rank, whose dress betokened his connection with the Papal Court.

The confessor, a monk of low, stout
stature and sensual aspect, was the last of
the group.

"Marquis," said the Marchioness, anti-
cipating him, "I am in agony; I feel as if
I were devoured by rats, and then as if
flames of fire were burning me in the bed.
I have had it slung in the air, but the fiend
haunts me still. The holy oil with which
our confessor has anointed me has brought
no ease, nor yet this blessed crucifix. I
suffer the pains of hell in body and mind."

"Marchesa," replied the general,
"there is not a better Catholic than you

in Italy; you have done enough to merit heaven without the intercession of St. Francis or St. Dominic, or any other saint in the calendar."

"Nay, you mock me. I feel that I have done nothing to what I might have done."

"No woman in Italy has done more. Have you not established the Holy Office of the Propaganda at Turin, and presided at its female branch?"

"But I feel that I have not done enough; my conscience upbraids me. Oh, but I would give my broad acres on the Mincio to die in peace like the poor vine-dresser, and to have a good hope of the kingdom of heaven."

"Illness hath overcome you. The absolution of our confessor should soothe your spirit, having shortened your time in purgatory."

"On his absolution I lean as a true Catholic, but death tests us strangely.

There is one pious act which my conscience urges, and which as death rests upon me I will not delay. Take this key, Pianesse, unlock my cabinet, and bring me what is in the second drawer on the left."

The Marquis did as requested, and lifting out a large velvet bag, he brought it to the Marchioness, who, stretching out her hand, drew it to her, and clasped it as it lay on the bed.

"Marquis, I have long toiled to exterminate heresy.   In vain have I endeavoured to uproot those rebels in the valleys near to Pignerol.   For this object I have collected the alms of the faithful, to which I have added a large portion of my own dowry. Take this bag, Pianesse; in it there are 6000 pistoles, besides some jewels, and promise me, as to a dying woman, that you will use this sum for the extirpation of these accursed heretics in the valleys of the Alps."

"I swear it by the Holy Mass.   Rest

in peace. I will convert the infernal brood, or blackened homesteads and bloody hearths shall prove the sincerity of my efforts."

"Thanks, Pianesse. My conscience needs appeasing. This blood will cleanse it from some stains. Take the money as my death tribute, as blood money, for which you are pledged to turn those three valleys into an Aceldama, unless the people go to mass, and adore our Immaculate Virgin. Count the money, and see that you have the full sum in gold, so that heaven may hold you responsible for the deed."

"Is that Echard whom I see there?" asked the Marchioness, turning towards the young officer.

"It is, mother; I mourn to see you thus suffering, and trust the Virgin may restore you to health. I have just returned from Rome, where I saw our holy father, Innocent X., and have brought his Apostolic blessing to the Duke, and to those who aid him."

"I receive it with thankfulness," said the Marchioness, crossing herself. " Echard, tell the Marquis to come near, for I feel the struggle approaching."

The Marquis advanced to the bed, and looked upon his wife's face as it became alternately livid and pale. " Holy Virgin," said he, bending on one knee, and holding the bag of gold in his hand, "help me to fulfil the death-wish of thy servant. Yes," exclaimed he, rising to his feet, " I will root up those apostates who stain the holy soil of Italy. The Pelice shall run with blood, and the stones of La Tour become crimsoned, so that the river shall not cleanse them, before I will flinch from the execution of this solemn charge."

" Wife," said the Marquis, " here is Gastaldo, the Papal delegate. We will begin now to carry out your wishes."

" My Lord, bring hither your parchment. Here is an edict ordering all those outside the three main valleys to quit their homes in

three days, under the penalty of confiscation
of goods and of death, unless they attend
mass. I think that is a move in the right
direction."

A faint smile passed over the dying
woman's features, and she moved her lips
to express assent.

" Quick, Echard, fetch that table, with
the pen and ink. Look, Marchioness, this
deed will turn thousands out of their homes
in this wintry month, and must bring forth
fruit. He shall sign it now before you, for
I have full powers from the Duke, and
Echard shall take and enforce it in the
valleys forthwith. Here, Signor Gastaldo,
here is the ink."

" May this gentle admonition on the
part of the Holy Mother Church bring
many of our strayed yet beloved children
back to our arms!" said the sleek delegate,
taking the pen, and adding the fatal hand-
writing to the deed.

" There, Marquis, there is the signature,"

added Gastaldo, "but I'll date it from Lucerna, when it is issued."

" Andrea Gastaldo, *Auditore è Delegato,*" glistened on the scroll, and the drying sand was sprinkled over the autograph.

That pen had inflicted more ruthless devastation than the sword; that drop of ink had traced a signature in which was hidden a volume of cruelty. It was but a name in ink, but it had power to break up loving families, and to drive them forth as exiles from their fathers' homes in the midst of winter.

"Look, Marchioness," said Pianesse, holding up the order before her glazing eye, that she might read the writing; "the deed is signed. It will bring forth fruit; if not, we will employ your treasure to good effect."

"Oh, kill the *barbets,*" screamed the sufferer, who was relapsing into another paroxysm—"kill them, Marquis.—Gastaldo, did you sign the order ?—Turn them out.

—Iolande, what are you doing?—Can't you rend that household?—Echard, take the order.—Your sword can do us service. —Marquis, spend the money. Oh the fire, the fire! I feel it again. My feet are scorched; the coverlet is on flames; quench it. The rats are eating my fingers. Take them off, inhuman monsters, who see me suffering, and yet do nothing."

"Lift up my bed, Marquis; do you hear? Hoist it up, or I'll curse you with my dying breath."

The Marquis seized one rope, and bidding Echard steady the bed, he, with the help of the attendant, raised it several feet from the ground.

"By all the seven Popes of Avignon," muttered the Abbot to himself, "I never saw anything like this before. I question whether any of our Popes had a harder death than this."

"Can't it go higher?" groaned the lady.

"I don't touch the rafter yet.—Are

your pullies right?—Malvicino—Echard—Iolande."

The dusk of evening had spread a gloom over the room, which was only relieved by the smouldering logs upon an open grate, common to the baronial castles of feudal times.

The flame flickered fitfully. Now it lit up the groups on the arras, and then, glancing from the gilded coronet, sank for some time, making the gloom more sensibly felt.

The breathing of the Marchioness became heavier, and her gasps more audible.

She writhed in the bed, which swayed to and fro with her movements. Horror was graven on her face, and the sweat stood in drops on that ghastly brow.

" Oh the fire! save me from the fire ;—quench it with blood.—Queen of heaven, Mother of God,—receive my soul.—For the sake of what I have now done,—relieve my torments.—Oh! the flames have encircled

my bed, my soul is on fire.—Oh, marquis,
spend the money—as—as I—said—let—
blood—be—shed—help the Holy Office,—
let the blood—of the *barbets* be shed—
blood——"

*   *   *   *   *   *

A convulsive gurgle, a rattle in the
throat, and all is silent—the Marchioness
is dead.

There lay the body, the grey tresses
dishevelled, the arms flung backwards, the
protruding eye staring into vacancy, the lips
unclosed.   The corpse became gradually
cold as it lay in the couch which still rocked
between heaven and earth in motion from
her dying spasm.

"Echard," said the Marquis, "thou shalt
witness how faithfully this blood-money
is expended, and according to thy mother's
dying wish, thou shalt specially assist in
fulfilling her last intentions."

Echard was silent. He brushed away
the falling tear, as he looked upon the

corpse of her he had addressed as mother; but, nevertheless, the scene caused his heart to tremble, as doing violence to his moral feelings, and, notwithstanding his natural prejudices, filled his conscience with disquieting reflections.

It was solemn to behold that chilled form, whose eyes still stared as if to pierce the veil of death, whose lips were not yet closed; it was solemn to remember that their last words were "blood," that she had bequeathed gold for the destruction of human life, and the infliction of misery on those whose sole crime was difference of faith.

Such was the dying bequest of the President of the Female Propaganda of Turin. Such were the last moments of the Marchioness of Pianesse. But her spirit has gone. We can trace her no farther. Her works follow her, and to her own Master she standeth or falleth, who will judge all according to their deeds.

CHAPTER XII.

THE BARBA.

THE sun was descending behind the hills in the direction of France, and its last beams glanced among the leafless branches of the chestnuts and walnuts at the entrance of the valley of Lucerna.

The children of the farm had crowded in the archway to witness that glorious sight in nature's drama, which untaught infancy appreciates as if by instinct, and the little ones had poured forth their joyous exclamations until the glowing orb became intercepted by the barrier of the Alps, whose broken ridges might be traced in rugged outline against the tinted sky.

"What a beautiful evening !" exclaimed Etienne, "and how clearly we see all the view. We shall have to go to grandfather directly, but I will see if I recollect the lesson Ardoine taught me. Come, Valère, help me."

"Well, those houses in front of us are those of Lucerna, and that white speck to the left is Lucernetta."

"Stop !" said Valère, "begin at the left."

"Those hills quite to our left, or south-west as Ardy calls it, are the Maritime Alps, and those peaks with that white mass of snow is Monte Viso."

"No," exclaimed Bertin, with some glee, "you are wrong; we can't see Monte Viso from here. You've forgotten it. I remember the name; those are the Alps de Bagnol—are they not, Laurent ?"

"Yes, you are right," replied the other.

"Then comes the slope," exclaimed André, "behind which Rora lies; look !

there's the bend on the top, near Pian Pra.
How brightly the snow shines in the setting
sun !"

"Straight before us," said Bertin, "is
the valley of Lucerna; the smoke of La
Tour is in the foreground, and at the foot
of that spur to the right is Villar. I can
see the hills above Bobi, and right at the
end, in the clouds, is Le Pra."

"We now get to the right side of the
valley that is on our right hand. There,"
said Revel, "is Castelluzzo, with his
curious hump. I always feel so glad
when I get a sight of it when I am away,
for I know then that I am getting near
home."

"I think," said Etienne, "little Lena
can tell me what this valley is running up
to the right."

"Angrogna," said the child, with a
smile.

"Look, André," said Etienne, "at that
floating bit of cloud over La Vachère; is

it not beautiful ?   I wish grandfather could see it, for he would admire it so much."

"Come, finish our semicircle. Quite to our right is La Costières, of St. Jean, and up there is that rock where we have been to play, and which has such a pretty view, Roccamanaut. But grandfather will be ready for us soon; let us go in and listen to Raynald until our turn comes."

"What are the two points," said Rodolphe to Raynald, as the children entered, "in which we glory ?"

"In our antiquity and purity."

"What do you mean by these ?"

"On the one hand, that we have been here from time immemorial, from the time that our ancestors received the truth from the apostles themselves, and on the other that we are primitive Protestants, ever opposed to the innovations of the Church of Rome. We are an unreformed church, and in this differ from the reformed churches of Germany."

" Are we, then, justly branded as heretics or schismatics ?"

" No, we are not a new church, we continue to be what we have been since the days of the apostles. Until the seventh century, no vital error had been introduced into the church, and we formed part of the church universal. When errors crept in our ancestors would not admit them, and their ministers did not on that account cease to be successors of those established by the apostles. To persevere, without interruption from the time of the apostles, in the pure doctrine they taught cannot surely be schism."

" Where should you say the true church of Christ was to be found after the heresies avowed at the second Council of Nice in 787 ?"

" In the churches of the valleys of Piedmont, for whose reformation history assigns no date; they were presided over by Claude, Bishop of Turin, who flourished in 817, and zealously protested against the introduction of images into places of worship."

"What tribute to our antiquity and purity can you derive from the writings of our opponents?"

"Reinerius Sacco, an inquisitor, who lived eighty years after Waldo of Lyons, admits that we flourished five hundred years before him; and Rorengo, who is now living, and is a neighbour of ours at Lucerna, allows in his last work that we preserve the opinions which Claude held in the ninth century."

"Can you tell me the names of some of the early reformers in the other parts of Europe?"

"Berenger, Peter de Bruys, Henry de Bruys, Arnulph, Arnold de Brescia, Huss, Jerome, Wickliffe, and others."

"Can you tell me some of the persecutions which the Popes of Rome have incited?"

"In 1179, Alexander III. issued a Bull against us, and in 1215 Innocent III. did the same, in which last crusade the Inquisitor Dominic earned his canonization. Also Innocent IV., Alexander IV., Urban IV., Innocent VIII., John XXII., Clement VII., and others, have done so."

"Can you mention some of the leading errors of the Church of Rome, with the date of their introduction?"

"The practice of confession, which was first authorized by a Lateran council, under Innocent III., in 1215. The worship of images, sanctioned by the second council of Nice, 787. Supremacy of the pope, in 606. Transubstantiation introduced in 818, and proclaimed an article of faith, under Innocent III., in 1215. The cup withheld from the laity, sanctioned first by the Council of Constance, in 1414; and purgatory, which received its present moulding principally from Aquinas, in the thirteenth century."

"Enough, my boy, you will confuse your old grandfather's head with so many figures—*Macte Virtute!* I am, however, much gratified with your application. I see you do more than count your sheep when you are on the hill-side. God grant you may know the power of the truth in your own experience, so that you may worthily hand on to others the pure word of God."

"Come, Etienne," said Rodolphe, stroking his head, "you will say your catechism well to-day, my boy. When was this catechism composed?"

"By our Barbas, in the twelfth century, grandfather."

"Right; so the same truth descends from father to child, as it is written, 'they shall declare the truth from one generation to another.' Where did we leave off?"

"At section three."

" ' What is the foundation of these commandments, by which every one ought to

enter into life ; without which foundation
the commandments cannot be worthily
kept nor accomplished ?' "

" ' The Lord Jesus Christ,' " replied
Etienne, in a grave tone, " ' of whom the
apostle says, 1 Cor. iii., ' For other foundation can no man lay than that is laid,
which is Jesus Christ.' "

" ' By what can man come to this foundation ?' "

" ' By faith. St. Peter saying, ' Behold,
I lay in Sion a chief corner stone, elect,
precious ; and he that believeth on Him shall
not be confounded.' And the Lord says,
' He who believeth in Me, hath eternal life.' "

" In what way can you know that you
believe ?"

" In that I acknowledge Him, Himself,
as very God and very man, who was
born and suffered for my redemption
and justification. In that I love Him,
Himself, and desire to fulfil his commandments."

" By what means does one arrive at the essential virtues, viz., faith, hope, and charity ?"

" By the gifts of the Holy Spirit."

" Dost thou believe in the Holy Spirit?"

" I believe in Him ; for the Holy Spirit, proceeding from the Father and the Son, is one person of the Trinity ; and as to divinity, is equal to the Father and the Son."

" Believest thou God the Father, God the Son, and God the Holy Spirit, to be three in person (three persons), then thou hast three Gods ?"

" There are not three (Gods)."

" Yet thou hast named three."

" That is by reason of the difference of the persons, not by reason of the essence of the divinity, for as there are three in person (three persons), so there is one in essence."

" Now, Claude, where are you, my boy ?"

"I am in section vii., beginning there. I have only learnt three, for I forgot it until last night."

"That's a little man, always speak the truth, and then it is easy to forgive you. The three you have learnt are very beautiful."

"On what account does one expect grace?"

"On account of the Mediator, Jesus Christ, of whom St. John says, 'Grace is come through Jesus Christ.' Also, 'We regard his glory full of grace and truth.' And, 'We have all received of his abundance.'"

"What is this grace?"

"It is redemption, remission of sins, justification, adoption, and sanctification."

"Through what do we hope for this grace in Christ?"

"Through living faith and true repentance, Christ saying, 'Repent ye, and believe the gospel.'"

"That will do very well, my little lad,"

said his grandfather, patting him on the head. "Now run to your mother, and tell her that you are a good boy, and don't forget to thank Aunt Marie, who takes such trouble with you, and hears your lesson as she lies upon her sick bed."

"Valère," said Rodolphe, "you have long learned your catechism, and I hope you have not forgotten it. Let me ask you the last question. In what does eternal life consist?"

"In a living and efficacious faith, and perseverance in the same," replied the boy unhesitatingly, as his eye brightened at his grandfather's appeal. "The Saviour says, John xvii. 3, 'And this is life eternal, that they might know Thee, the only true God, and Jesus Christ whom Thou hast sent;' and he who shall persevere in this to the end, he shall be saved. Amen."

"I am pleased that you remember so well. When we have once learned any-thing it is a pity to forget it, for very little attention enables us to retain what we have mastered."

"Now, grandfather," said Etienne, " now that we have said our catechism, tell us one of your stories."

" Tell us something about the plague," said Bertin.

"No," said Claude, clambering upon his grandfather's knee, " let us not hear about that till Ardy comes. Tell us about the great fire which lasted so many days, not long after the plague, and burnt up so many leagues and all the woods, when they tried to put out the flames with wine instead of water."

" Ah !" said the old man, " I lived then in a cottage over in Angrogna, and could see the fire on the side of Lucerna. The mountain was like a sea of flame. We could see the glowing waves ascending the hill, when all behind was black ; and it was several days before they reached the highest row of pines. But I think you

have heard this before; I will tell you
what my grandfather used to tell me, when
I was a boy. Some of you may grow up
and may have to do like things in your
days. I used to sit by him and play with
his stick, spectacles, and ring as you do,
Etienne, with mine; and then, when I was
too noisy, he used to tell me what he had
seen when he was young."

"Oh do tell me, grandfather, for I
should like to hear, and then I shall be
quiet too."

"I will, my boy, for God only knows
whether you may take part in a similar
scene. It was in the year 1561."

"That was nearly a hundred years ago,
was it not?"

"Yes, within six years. Well, news
came that Francis I. of France was dead;
so deputies were sent from this valley, by
way of Bobi, to meet those of the Val
Clusone, to renew the league of support
between the valleys of Piedmont and those

of Dauphiny. It was on the twenty-first
of January, in the middle of winter, as it
is now, that the deputies returned across
the Col Julien in a tremendous snow-
storm."

"And were any of them lost in the
snow?" asked little Renée.

"No; they arrived near Bobi, and then
their friends met them to tell them that an
edict had been passed in their absence, to
compel them to appear before a council
of war next morning, 'to know whether they
would go to mass or not.'"

"And what was to be done to them if
they did not go?" said Etienne, whose im-
patience would not allow his grandfather to
proceed without interruption.

"They were to be sent to the galleys
like felons, or to be burnt alive at the
stake; and they had one night given to
them to decide what they would do."

"And is that what they would do to us
now? What did your grandfather do, then?"

" They all knelt down and prayed to God
to help them—not one of them would give
up his religion, or the truths of that catechism which you have just been learning;
but they could not get away, for it was
winter, and the snow had blocked up all
the passes."

" What did they do then ?"

" They resolved to defend themselves,
or die in defence of their religion. They
raised their hands to heaven, and vowed
they would assemble, as before, in their
own place of worship. So next day they
all went to the temple at Bobi for service,
and then came out to face the enemy."

" And did your grandfather fight ?"

" They all had to fight, and our brave
fathers drove the Papists to the citadel of
Villar, where, after a siege of ten days,
they made them all prisoners."

" And they did all that a hundred years
ago, when the snow was on the ground as
it is now ?"

" Yes ; and think what a solemn night that must have been, when they had to decide what they would do ; and how earnestly they must have prayed to God for direction and courage, when this great danger was before their faces."

"Oh, it was glorious," said the little fellow, clapping his hands. "I'm glad I had a grandfather there."

" Quick, I think I hear Aunt Lucille calling us to supper."

CHAPTER XIII.

THE apartment in which the family assembled for their evening repast was the largest in La Baudène, and its arrangements displayed more comfort and resources than were generally met with among the poor peasants of the valleys.

The floor of the room was flagged. Down the centre ran a long oaken table, on either side of which were ranged rows of stiff high-backed chairs. Across the horizontal beams forming the base of the triangular roof were laid long poles, on which loaves of bread and other articles were placed, while at either end frames containing numerous spindles of home-spun thread were suspended by strings. Well scoured vessels for milk were neatly arranged above the cheese presses and wooden churns, pleasant tributes to Lucille's thrift and management, while implements of husbandry and spinning-wheels indicated that the family did not eat the bread of idleness. In one corner stood a large frame for weaving, for, as is still the case in the Norwegian *bonde's* cottage, division of labour was little understood, and most of the articles of domestic use were of home manufacture. The board was plentifully supplied, for though the valleys had been much impoverished by their forced contributions to maintain a squadron of Savoy and the French regiments of Grancey, still the prudent management of the sisters did not suffer the household of La Baudène to lack.

Rye bread, with butter and cheese, filberts, chestnuts, fish, and milk, formed the staple of the repast. Knives and forks, plates and dishes, of the coarsest workmanship, were duly laid upon the clean white cloth, a luxury still found in the humblest albergo, although a barren compensation for the mediocrity of the Italian *cuisine*.

The table was arranged in sets, each father and mother being the centre of their group. A patriarchal sight it was when the board was full, a sight which has rarely been seen on earth, and possibly has been seen nowhere else save in the farm of La Baudène.

"Come sisters," said Lucille, as she threw some wood on the embers, and cast in some more chestnuts, "our evening meal is ready. Madeleine has milked Brunon, and our little people are impatient to begin. Come, for we like to send our darlings to rest soon after sunset."

"Here, Valère, we want some more salt. There is the mortar, now let me see if you can pound us some by the time we are seated."

"Oh yes, aunt, I like that sort of work," replied the lad, "better than doing what suits the girls."

"Oh! Ardoine, I have burnt my fingers," cried Etienne, who had been trying to remove the iron pot which hung over the wood fire, supported by a large hook, on a primitive chain.

"Never mind," said Ardoine, "you shall taste our new apple wine, with some sugar. Now drive out the hens, and put those sieves and baskets in their places."

"My poor Barthélemy," said Lucille, speaking of her boy, who was a colporteur, "he's been away nearly five months, but he was to return to-day. You see I have laid his plate, so I had not forgotten him."

"Yes," said Ardoine, "it was about the time when Raynald went out harvesting in the plains, as we were permitted to do by the Duke's edict of last May."

"You may take your places," said Lucille, "but we will not begin until all are ready."

"Take your places quietly, children," whispered Ardoine.

"We are coming, Lucille," said Janavel; "your cheerful face is a grace to our repast, and to your industry we are indebted for the variety which adorns our board."

"There is little enough of that; we are but Alpine peasants, but we bless God for what we have, and eat our bread with thankfulness."

"Valère, my boy, how have you sped to-day in your labours in that new field? Those numerous stones and weeds will tax your strength and patience."

"I have done well; for I have had the pleasure of my mother's company. She sat upon a stone which is in the middle of the field, and defies my efforts, and there she chanted the hymns which soothe Aunt

Marie; and under her eye I could not but labour with heart and soul."

"Well, vine-dresser," said Janavel, addressing Laurent, "yours is dreary work in January.   Can you find employment for the day?"

"Yes, father, digging the soil is part of our work, as well as pruning the berries; but the weather is not so pleasant as when I brought the basket of first fruits to Aunt Marie."

"Dear sister," said Renée, "what sort of a day has she passed? I was hoping she would feel well enough to hear me sing that air which she loves so much."

"Oh, do sing for us, Aunt Renée," cried little Susanne, "you said you would if we were good children, and I and five of my cousins have been playing together all day, and we have tried to remember what you said about kind words, and have not quarrelled once."

"Good child," said Renée, as she

stooped, and smoothing off the child's hair
from her forehead, kissed her; " you shall
sit near me at table this evening, and have
something out of aunt's basin."

" Here comes Aline," said Madeleine;
" she has just said good-night to her pet
sheep; look how she holds our old dog
Liberta by the ear; look, André, he wags
his tail as if he were quite pleased."

" Etienne," said Lucille, " set chairs
round the table, and put grandfather's glass
in its proper place; you know he is pleased
with these little attentions, and it is the
duty of children to please their elders."

" I had not forgotten," replied the boy,
" I remember his kind smile, how he patted
my head, and said a verse, I think it was
out of the Old Testament; I should know
it again if I heard it."

" Marguerite," said Madeleine, " have
you placed my seat next yours? you know
I cannot enjoy a meal unless I am at your
side."

"Our little friends will not forget what each person likes, and will do their best to please all. We want all to be happy, don't we, Etienne?"

"I am sure we do. Grandfather says smiles are like sunbeams, and it is so nice to see those we love happy. I wish I could make mother happy, I do love her; but she only cries when I try to please her, and seems as if she could not smile."

"Oh, sweet home," sang Lucille, as she moved about, now turning the chestnuts, now mixing the curds, now arranging the honey. "Sweet home, there's no place like home."

"Come, Susanne, take away this knife, and don't play with uncle's silver cup. You know how much he values it, for it was given him by the Duke when he took refuge in our farm many years ago."

"And how are your goats?" said Marguerite to young Revel; "I hope you had not to chase your truants far to-day."

" No, mother, they felt tired after yesterday's run, for they led me a chase to the path which branches off to the cavern in the Vandalin. It is not often they want driving, for they know my voice and follow me about; to-day even old Grey-beard ate out of my hand quite quietly."

"And did you remember," said his mother, " to repeat your catechism over while you were watching your flocks? I reminded you how David used to think upon God, and compose his Psalms on the mountain."

" I did not forget it," said the boy, " I shall be able, I hope, to say it perfectly when you question me next time."

The little Aline sat in her chair patiently awaiting the commencement of the repast. The mother, who was secretly admiring her child, could restrain herself no longer; she bent over her and kissed her forehead, saying to herself—

" My little darling, you might have been

one taken to Duke Philip VII., and he would have seen that what our enemies said about our having one eye in the middle of the forehead, and four rows of black teeth were wicked lies, for you are the greatest beauty in the plains of Piedmont, that you are; yes, that you are, though mother says it."

Rodolphe and Janavel now entered, and the old man seated himself at the head of the table. The whole family stood up while the aged grandfather, with closed eyes and clasped hands, asked a blessing on their repast.

For a moment there was silence throughout the room, while the patriarchal family acknowledged the Giver of all good gifts, and worshipped the God of their fathers.

The silence was broken by shouts in the distance, and the clatter of horses' hoofs against the paved road grew more and more distinct. It was clear that a body of men were galloping up the avenue.

Janavel exchanged glances with Rodolphe as he listened to the sound, doubting
whether it might be a band of the brigands
in the pay of the Abbey of Pignerol, or a
company of the Duke's soldiers, who were
quartered in the valley. They were not, however, left long in doubt. A violent knocking
was heard at the outer gate, which was
burst open, and eighteen or twenty men in
French uniform galloped into the courtyard.

"Now then," said one of the men,
"where's our new landlord? Old fellow,
we've come to lodge and sleep. Here's
your Duke's orders to billet us on you."

"We have not much room," replied
Rodolphe, calmly, "but we are always glad
to carry out our Duke's wishes. We therefore welcome our guests, and will do what
we can to make them comfortable."

"But where are we to put them
all?" said Lucille in an under tone; "with
our numerous family our house is already
crowded."

"I must leave that to you, Lucille, you are the housekeeper, and know the family arrangements. We must not mind a little discomfort, as our Sovereign wishes this proof of our loyalty."

"Come, is supper ready?" shouted out one of the men. "I'm hungry, and we know the proverb here," continued he, singing in a rollicking voice—

> "Chi va a letto senza cena,
>   Tutta notte si dimena."

"Old man, we'll save you from the gout, and you know that he who steals an old man's supper does him no wrong. But I see a cloth. Here's the feast ready laid for us. This way, boys. Corporal, take the top." And the soldiers rushed into the dining-room, while the little children crouched behind their mothers, or made their escape as best they could.

CHAPTER XIV.

THE BILLET.

"Come, old landlord," said one of the soldiers, Berru by name, "a glass of your old vintage. What's he got in his cellar? we'll be content with the Pope's *Monte Pulciano*."

"Fetch out your oldest brew," shouted Dagot, brandishing his sword, and driving it through a loaf which stood on the table.

"Here's a bottle of something. It looks too thick, as if ——. Ah! the wine itself smells of heresy," said the man, putting the bottle to his nose.

"It's like vinegar. Come here, young fellow," said he, addressing Etienne, "and

I'll wash your head with it like a good nurse."

"Take your places," cried the corporal, "we have not always such bright waiters."

"Here, my fair lass," said he, turning to Ardoine, "mix my drink, sugar it well; make it sweet, like yourself. I pledge your health, and wish you the man of your heart —heart, oh."

"Landlord," cried Berru, "I want a pair of shoes; I hope you keep a good supply. Here, you with the straight nose and black eyes, take my measure," said he, stretching out his legs, and addressing Marguerite; "go and see if your husband's shoes will fit me, for you see I limp. Girls, get your knitting ready, for you shall knit my garters."

"What a stroke of fortune to find supper waiting for us! You expected us, then, and would have been disappointed if we had not turned up; more sugar, my golden lass. Will you smile on a wandering soldier? If I knew who your lover was, I'd spit him, for I'll have no rival."

"Look out, boy," said Berru, taking a cup, and flinging it at Valere's head.

The boy escaped the blow, but the cup dashed against the wall, and lay shivered on the floor.

"Friends and brethren in arms," said the corporal, standing at one end of the table, and steadying himself by leaning one hand on Dagot's shoulder; "friends, I'm highly honoured. You are, I mean—You've got some of the soldiers of his most Christian Majesty, Louis—I forget his number— I try to recollect it as I was taught in school. Twice seven are thirteen—no. fourteen; that's it. You must make us comfortable. I drink your health, old sexton in the corner. A toast for his Majesty the Pope. Open your mouths, boys. We're come here to keep you at peace and to protect you, to convert you. Look at this bright blade of mine; it's brought two

or three into the fold—and—where was I?
and taught them to say an *Ave* with the true
accent."

"What's that old woman all in black
for?" cried Berru, grasping Martha by the
arm.

"Come now," said Mullenier, "com-
rades, you should not insult these good
people who are willing to do their best for
us. Let her go, Berru, or you and I shall
see who has learned his drill best. Go,
go, mistress," said he in an under tone to
Martha.

The corporal raised himself in his chair,
and looked round the room. "Girl," said
he, addressing Ardoine, "will you accept
me for a partner?—let us have a dance—I
can't keep my legs."

So saying, he dragged the cloth off the
table, and knives, plates, mugs, eatables,
lay in one mingled confusion on the floor.

"Beg pardon, old sexton, if I trod on
your corns. This fellow, boys, has the eye

of a *barbet*. We must convert him. I'll hear his doctrine, he shall preach to us. We'll rig him up."

"Here's his cap," said Dagot, placing a large earthen basin on Rodolphe's head.

"A gown; here tie the table-cloth round his neck."

Ardoine could resist no longer. Rushing forward, she seized the basin, and dashed it to the ground, and casting herself between the soldiers and her grandfather, exclaimed—

"You call yourselves men. You can ill-treat women, and insult old age. Shame on you! Have none of you fathers? Have you seen no grey hairs in your own mother's head that should teach you to respect the grey hairs of an old man? Are none of you fathers, and has the sound of a child's voice never caused your hearts to beat with pity, you who now seem like fiends in the midst of an innocent family? God of heaven!" she exclaimed, as she clasped her hands, and looked up, "be not far from us. Deliver us from the fury of these men, and send help for thy name's sake."

Her aspect was such as might arrest the murderer.

Those soldiers from a foreign land felt the majesty of woman's excellence, and yielded that homage that virtue extorts from the wicked themselves.

That artless girl had caught the inspiration of an impulsive heroism from the mountain storm and free air of her native glens. In her self-forgetful anxiety for her grandfather, she who at first quailed at the sound of the soldiers' voice, and shrank behind Rodolphe's chair, boldly confronted the tried veterans of many a battle-field.

These men paused as they beheld her eyes flashing, and the escaped tresses of golden hair flowing over her shoulders, feeling a passing admiration for such devoted

affection and disregard of danger. She
laid one hand on Rodolphe, and stretching
out the other to repel the assailants,
looked with intrepid dignity upon the
crowd of rugged faces by whom she was
surrounded. For a moment all seemed
conscience stricken.

"Stand back," said Mullenier, "the girl's
right; I'll fight for her single-handed.
Back, I say, or I'll mix the blood of some
of you with the wine that's on this
floor, and see which is thickest and
reddest."

"You want to get the girl for yourself,"
said Dagot. "That's what he's after, com-
rades. You swore that the next prize
should be mine, and I claim this one.
Honour among brethren;" so saying he
rushed upon Mullenier. Their swords clashed
fiercely, and the clang of the metal ,was
heard high above the shouts and cries of
the lawless throng. Life would probably
have been lost in the tumult, had not Du

Petit Bourg, the officer of the men, suddenly entered—

"Shame—shame, Frenchmen. Is this military order ? We are soldiers and not brigands. To your quarters this moment. What a wreck you have made of this place! If you would fare well, treat these honest people well, and do not rob them in their home. To your quarters at the other side of the court. Quick, or I'll order fifty lashes for the man that's last in this room."

"Here, Mullenier, do what you can to set things to rights. Come, my good people, do not be alarmed, no one shall hurt you. Father," said he, addressing Rodolphe, "I am sorry to incommode you, I will do my best to keep my men out of your way. There, now, things are a little better. It seems a mockery to bid you continue your meal; but rest on my honour, this brave girl shall have no cause to fear for her grandfather, nor for the little ones whom I see trembling in the corner. Good evening, my friends." So saying, the officer bowed and retired.

CHAPTER XV.

THE inhabitants of the valleys had suffered for some time past from the settlement of missionary monks and the cantonment of troops, and had had for some years a regiment of Savoy annually forced upon them, whose period of winter quarters often extended to ten months.

In addition to these, at the time of which we are now treating, (the Duchess of Savoy having made arrangements with the minister of Louis XIV., Cardinal Mazarin,) the troops of Marshal Grancey had wintered in the valleys. They consisted of the regiments of Navarre, Quincé, Altesse, and

Grancey, in all numbering three thousand men.

Of the last of these, Du Petit Bourg was First Captain.

The family of La Baudène had hitherto been strangely exempt from these inflictions, considering their position and number, and it was not until the incident related in the previous chapter that they felt this cruel inroad on their domestic peace, and this drain on their resources.

Du Petit Bourg, however, used every effort to alleviate the oppressive tax, and his endeavours were successful. Not many days had passed before a marked difference was perceptible in the bearing of the men.

The wondrous unity, the patriarchal simplicity, the genuine kindness of the family, had, by dint of sheer moral force, won a way to their hearts. Their uproarious songs were comparatively hushed, and no personal outrages were offered to any of the family. One man only had still a scowl on his face.

Ardoine's presence acted on them like the spring sunshine after the morning rain, and if old Rodolphe passed, some of them would involuntarily rise to do homage to the hoary head. Even the little children found playmates among the weather-beaten warriors of Gaul.

"Well, messieurs," said Mullenier, one morning, as he watched Ardoine bringing her grandfather's glass of spring water, "In all our wanderings we've not seen such a family as this. They are more like what we used to read of in books when we were young, than what we have met with in our knocking about the world."

"It really is," answered Lenois, "it's a pity they are heretics."

"Heretics or saints, did you ever find as good a lot of Catholics? come, confess. It reminds me of my early days when I lived with my dear mother in Southern

Languedoc," continued the speaker, brushing away a tear from his eye. "There were some near us who were of this way of thinking, and good honest folks they were."

"One feels a sort of peace here," interposed Parelles, "which even fellows like us who dabble in blood are glad to enjoy."

"I only say it's a pity they're heretics," doggedly retorted his companion; "however well they may have done in this world, they will be lost in the next."

"God may be more merciful than the Pope," rejoined his companion, "but I say, judge them by their fruits. Why, look at our men, did you ever see them so quiet before? It's an awful tax to have us here, and yet how civil and hospitable they've been."

"Here, boy," said Mullenier, hailing Etienne, "who's that just come into the yard? I think I've seen him somewhere."

"That's Pastor Léger, the Moderator

of our Churches, what grandfather once was, when he was younger."

"Ah! now I recollect—*Santo Bambino!* that's the man that caught hold of the tail of the Captain's horse and rushed into our lines, as we were about to march into La Tour some months back."

"Ha, ha," said Parelles, "that was a brave act. Though I felt inclined to split when I saw the old fellow flying like a cat over a hot oven. They are a brave people, and no mistake."

"But they're heretics, and will be damned," doggedly remarked Lenois.

"Come, don't be so hard on them, because they're heretics," replied Parelles; "look at their fruits. You've come from Rome, Mullenier, did you ever see as much good there in the holy city of the Pope and the cardinals?"

"No," answered the soldier, "although it's full of holy bones and teeth. The dead are holy with a vengeance, but as for the living, leave no room for saints in your calendar, Peter, for there are no applicants there now-a-days. I heard say there, that you could do what you like if you would only pay. There's a regular tax for sin, at least it used to be so, when the Pope got rich by other's sins, and kept a bureau open for the convenience of sinners."

"Come, you must have had the nightmare, and that has made you bilious; but let's hear what you did see there."

"See, why it would take me a week to describe the sights of Rome. I have a good knowledge of the *Scala Santa*, and shan't forget that till my knees get well."

"What is that?"

"It is a staircase of twenty-eight marble steps, which belonged to Pilate's house, and down which our Saviour walked when he left the judgment seat. No one is allowed to walk up it."

"Then how did you get to the top?"

"On my marrow-bones. To save my

soul, I rubbed off all the skin of my
knees; but for all the spiritual good it did
me, I might as well try to cure my tooth-
ache with a violin. There were sixty of us
shuffling up bowing and kissing, and the
old woman before me was rather awkward
at the new work, for she kept hitting my
nose with her foot as she moved up a
step."

" I'll bet you were thinking what she
was like, in the midst of your prayers.
Confess now."

" Come, comrade, don't play the priest;
I might have debated it when I saw the
foot, but when she looked round—*Santo
Bambino!* her face made me pray twice as
hard to the Holy Mother to keep me from
the evil eye."

" Now if she was as good-looking as
the girl here, then I know you'd have
clipped your prayers and left the Virgin to
finish her *Ave* herself. That brute Dagot
how he dodges her; it seems as if he were

after mischief; I hope Du Petit Bourg will keep his eye on him."

"I'll forfeit this cap, which I had on when Innocent blessed us, or my *Scala Santa* leggins, but I should not wish harm to come to this lot."

"But talking of your *scala*, I suppose you earned a good plenary indulgence? What did you get for each step?"

"Oh, if I remember rightly, nine years' indulgence; and well earned, grinding up on one's knees, kissing every step, and mumbling a *Pater* and an *Ave*."

"What do you mean by an indulgence? only nine years of it would not be worth the skinning!"

"Oh don't ask me points of faith, I don't know, and no one else. I never could find one yet who could tell me what it did mean. When I confessed at Rome I asked the friar especially about the indulgence, but he gave me some cloudy answer, that I was as wise as a bear in a bull-fight."

"Well, what else have you seen?"

"Oh I can't tell you, I forget. At Padua I recollect seeing old Anthony preaching to the fishes. He was a fine preacher, he was, but I should be sorry if our friar got a hint from him, for now if I can't sleep in bed I'm sure of a nap in church in Lent when I go. Why, man, the fishes were staring and opening their months, eels, turbots, flounders, soles, with their heads out of water, winking religiously and showing their teeth; and they've got many bits of him among their relics, as fresh as when he was alive, but I didn't see these."

"Ah!" replied his companion, "it's a fine thing to travel, it opens your mind and your mouth too. But hark! I hear the bugle. What does it mean? Here, Capet, come tell us our orders."

"The Captain talks of flitting," replied the man. "In an hour we are to march to Villar, up the valley, and I'm afraid we shall not get as good a supper as we do here, nor get our cheese toasted so brown."

"It's a bore," said Parelles, "to turn out, they've made us comfortable, and that old mother in black, and your favourite girl, knew exactly how much sugar to put into my drink. You admit this, don't you, Lenois?"

"Their kitchen," replied the dogged Lenois, "is better than their creed."

"Well," said Mullenier, "I suppose we must get ready. I'm sorry for ourselves, but glad for them, poor things. Would that the day might come when I could do any of them a good turn. Bless that girl, I'd risk something to serve her."

"Boy," cried Parelles, addressing Bertin, who was passing, "say good bye for us to your aunts, cousins, and grandfather. And now to horse in the name of our most Christian King, Louis XIV."

CHAPTER XVI.

AFTER the withdrawal of the soldiers billeted at La Baudène, the family circle had resumed their usual routine, and from the middle of the month had pursued their ordinary avocations without molestation.

It was on the evening of the 25th of January (a date still salient in the bloody chronicles of the Waldensian valleys) that Ardoine, having fulfilled her household duties, was tempted by the sunshine to visit her favourites in the meadow, near the Pelice. Having tied her kerchief loosely round her head, and thriftily taken her knitting apparatus to redeem the spare moments, she tripped gaily to the river side. The cattle lifted their heads, acknowledging in their brute instinct the presence of her whose hand caressed them, or gave them their dainty bit. Having thrown her arms round Brunon, and indulged in the expression of her artless affection, Ardoine began to ply her work, wandering on till she reached the Pelice.

Standing on the bank she watched the river as it eddied among the stones, now gliding in a glassy silent stream, in which the motion mocks the tracings of the eye; now broken into crested roaring foam, as some barrier of rock chafed the descending current; and then beyond relapsing once more into a motionless lake-like mirror.

She paused on coming to a spot where the stream ran deep and clear. Laying down her knitting implements, the maiden knelt upon the bank, and looked into the darkened yet crystal pool, as if she would count the glossy pebbles beneath. The

sun was shining, and its rays glanced on
the tremulous water, dappling the stony
bed beneath, which quivered in the wavy
light. Heaven and earth were friendly
to the maiden, for sun and water combined together to render homage to her
beauty.

Sketched upon the brittle stream the
girl beheld the image of herself. Her golden
tresses, her snowy brow, her dazzling eyes,
her minutest features, were reproduced as
in a glass. Bending forward she gazed
admiringly at the fairy likeness, and having
looked once, she would not have been true
to woman's instincts if she had not looked
again, with a more protracted gaze, at the
portrait wrought so simply, yet so exqui-
sitely, by Nature herself. Her feelings were
but the flitting thoughts of the moment,
the unconscious action of human nature.
After a moment's pause she dipped her
hand into the shallower water, and picking
up a pebble cast it into the glassy pool,

and smilingly watched the shivered portrait which was scattered upon the circling
ripples.

"Thou art marred," she exclaimed,
with a sigh, "thou frail type of human
life ! Now all is smooth, and hope smiles,
then some unforeseen blow comes, and
breaks the images of peace our hearts had
shapen unawares, and makes our bright
visions like yon disjointed portrait on the
troubled water."

She continued looking into the stream,
and watched the gradual relapse of the
ripples, until she saw the reflection of an
approaching figure, and turning beheld her
cousin Raynald.

"Welcome to the brook, dear Raynald,
is not this a bright sunshiny day for
January? It makes me feel quite fresh
after mother's sick room."

"It is bright, cousin, to those who
have no weight upon their heart; but to
those who have, nature's smiles seem

mockery, speaking of joys they cannot
find within."

"Cousin, cousin," said Ardoine, raising
her eyes, "what means this? Who should
be happier than you, young and strong,
the favourite of our home circle?"

"Ah! but there is one in that circle
whose smile I would strive to win; my
heart craves the companionship of one."

"Who is that, Raynald? It is hardly
right to prefer one to the others, for all
are delighted to have your company, and
look brightly when they hear your voice."

"Cannot you guess who it is I should
wish to have ever by my side, whose voice
I would fain hear chanting my *Ranz des
Vaches,* and under whose eye I would re-
view my fold?"

"I am sure there are many you would
like to have with you, for I know you are
not fond of being alone. There is Aunt
Lucille, who is so cheerful and good-
natured, and Aunt Renée, who sings

so sweetly; you would be glad to hear them sing as you pasture your flock on the mountain."

"Ardoine, I often think how happy I have been with you from childhood, how we have grown up together, and rambled over these hills side by side—you are part of my earliest and brightest memories. If you were gone from La Baudène, I am afraid I should find it a melancholy place."

"Oh, don't say so, Raynald; I am sure there would be a great many friends left, so you would not miss me long; but it is very kind of you, Raynald, to think thus."

"Ardoine, I have often been to Turin, and looked at the maidens in the city— many of them boast bright eyes and raven hair, but none ever make me forget your eyes, and I have never seen any who have such beautiful hair as yours."

"Dear Raynald, you are my cousin, and you think too kindly of me. Look at

this stream, the water has settled, you can
see my face quite naturally there; now
look, I am going to spoil the fine picture
with this stone."

"Oh don't, Ardoine," said the young
man, laying his hand on her arm; "I
can't have that face spoiled; even the very
water is my friend, and loves your face.
Would that I could have it ever before
me! If you could read my heart you would
see that picture which the water reflects
stamped there also. I have one great
desire, and that is to please you, and to do
what you wish. Will you let me please
you?"

" Let you please me ? of course I will.
I will tell you what I wish if it will give
you pleasure to do it. We should give
pleasure to others when we can, and I am
sure I ought to do so, to my kind and
favourite cousin."

" Dear Ardoine, I am afraid you do not
understand what I mean; I want you to

give me some great work to do, that I may
win your smile. It is strange, but one
kind word from you will make me do
wonders."

"But I trust, dear Raynald, that I am
always kind, at least I wish to be so ; I
would never say a cross word wilfully. If
I do, it is poor human nature. How could
I kneel down by mother's bed at night, if
I had said anything to vex you, or anybody
else ?"

" Oh, no, you would not grieve me, you
never do, you are always good and gentle ;
but when I come near you I become so
weak, and often begin to tremble. If I
think you are not happy a load comes upon
my heart, and I feel that I can do anything to
make you so ; and when you smile and look
on me, I want no other happiness than to
look at you and hope that you are thinking
of me."

" If that makes you happy then I am
sure you may be so. Do not I often look

at you every day, and think of you, too, when I say my prayers morning and evening? Well, after what you have said, Raynald, I shall try you; let me hear a verse of that song you sing when you call your goats in at eventide."

"Oh, dear cousin, excuse me, I can't sing; you must forgive me; my heart won't let me sing; if I tried I should be quite out of tune, and that would grate on your ear."

"What, are you so soon faithless to your promises? Oh, Raynald! Well, then, let me cheer you; I will sing you a verse which I know is your favourite."

So saying, without further preamble, Ardoine sang—

"Tout dort dans la nature,
    Un seul ruisseau murmure."

The young man gazed at her with the fixity of admiration and reverence as she poured forth her notes.

She was the anti-type of his unconscious day-dreams, the being that thrilled his life with purpose, and filled the restless void of his yearning heart. In her presence the dauntless mountaineer became a child, for the touch of her little finger could make him tremble from head to foot.

He drank in her song with silent rapture, but his expression was tinged with sorrow, and his changing colour betrayed his inward struggles. He listened with half-open lips, as if he dared not breathe, lest he should lose a syllable, but the involuntary sigh declared that the pleasure was allied to pain.

"There, Raynald," said the girl, throwing back her gleaming tresses, which had escaped from her kerchief, "I have been kinder than you. Come, my dear cousin, do not look so grave or sad, for I hope there is no gloomy news. Now we must go home, for I have been out a long time; mother will be wanting me, and we are both away from her, and grandfather will be waiting for his evening chapter to be read; the boys will want to hear a little story, and I must see if they know their verses, and it will soon be time to send the little ones to bed; so I think we must return. Now you may give me your hand to help me among these stones, and then I shall tell them all how kind and useful my dear cousin has been."

"Wait a moment, Ardoine," said Raynald, "I must run to the *chálet* and loose poor Liberta, whom I left tied up there. I shall not be long." So saying, he darted off, and was soon out of sight.

Ardoine resumed her knitting, humming to herself snatches of mountain songs, and looking from time to time into the flowing current. She stepped on some large stones which lay dry in the bed of the stream. She had not long been left alone before she heard footsteps, and turning round saw the French soldier, Dagot, one of those who had been billeted on the farm. She had always beheld his sinister expression with alarm and horror.

" Come, my pretty maid, I am lucky to find you alone, your bright eyes don't need candle-light. You have got a French soldier for a lover. I've been to Pavia, I've fought the Pope knows where," said the soldier, who stood between Ardoine and the bank.

" Sir," replied the girl, " I do not understand you ; were you not one of those who were lodged at our farm ? I trust you do not mean me ill."

" Mean you ill ? wedlock with a brave soldier of fortune is not an ill, you may do better with me than with some frowsy goatherd."

" I pray you leave me ; it is not the custom with us for men to waylay lonely girls ; leave me, if you have any of that honour of which the French are always boasting."

" Nay, nay, I could not leave you ; it is a chance of war to find you alone. You must come along with me," and the soldier stepped out on the stones.

"If you come nearer, I will leap into the river," replied Ardoine, with a convulsive shudder. "I should have thought a Frenchman would be ashamed to attack a poor girl."

" Come, my love," said Dagot, suddenly leaping forward ; seizing her by the wrist he dragged her from the stones towards the bank.

But an arm was lifted up to thwart his wicked purpose. A well-directed blow from behind struck him on the head. The soldier, entangled with his sword and musket, fell with a crash into the river, troubling the glassy pool which had so lately reflected that maiden's face.

Drenched to the skin he floundered in the water, which choked his half-expressed oaths and cries. The current was strong, but at length he grasped the roughness of the rock with the tips of his fingers, and succeeded in keeping his eyes and nose above the water.

"Come, Ardoine," said Raynald, "don't be frightened, take my arm. I will fetch you a drink in my hat. Don't be afraid, he'll not come again; his musket is wet, and he will have enough to do to keep himself afloat till somebody helps him out. If he comes again I'll not let him off so easily. Don't tremble, darling, forget all about it. I can see the farm before us, and some of the children are waiting for you. Thank God, all's well that ends well. Look, here's our true friend, Liberta; you'd mark his throat, old boy, if your mistress was in danger."

When Raynald felt that fragile arm resting on his, he thought that the reward was beyond the slight effort he had made, and that he could brave danger in its deadliest form could he but win one smile of encouragement from her he so ardently loved.

CHAPTER XVII.

THE PLAGUE.

DURING the same afternoon the family had been joined by the Moderator Léger, who was a frequent and a welcome guest at La Baudène.

"Well, Father Rodolphe," said the Moderator, as he entered, "I greet you, and my little ones; how are they all?"

"We are so glad to see you, Barba," said Etienne, "for we like to listen to your stories."

"Have you remembered what I told you last time about my uncle, who was at Constantinople, and knew the martyr Cyril Lucar, the Greek patriarch?"

"I remember that," said Etienne; "you said he was a Protestant in heart, and wrote a celebrated confession of faith."

"Uncle Léger," said Bertin, who had been reflecting for some time, "I hope you will not think me rude, but I want to know how it is you have broken that front tooth."

"I will tell you, my boy. Many years ago I was pastor of Roderet, and was overtaken in a snow-storm; my head was, as it were, frozen. I became so ill that I was given up as dead; my ears were swollen and my jaws locked, so to try to save me they broke one of my front teeth, and then they inserted a silver tube, and sustained life by pouring down some liquids."

"Thank you for telling me, Barba," said Bertin, satisfied with the explanation.

"The sight of you, friend Léger," said Rodolphe, "reminds me of times past when I was Moderator; troublous times they were, especially in 1630, the year of the plague."

"Oh, do tell us something about it, grandfather," said little Revel, "we all like to hear you relate anything that happened a long time ago."

"Well, well, dear children, if you like to listen to an old man's rambling on the past, you shall; for who knows," said he, sighing, "whether we shall often be able to meet in this way. Come round me, then, daughters and little ones, and let me refresh your memories."

"There, Aline and Lena, you can sit opposite one another, one on each knee, and sit very quietly while grandfather speaks," said Rodolphe, giving them each a kiss.

"Ah! I remember well the year 1629; it was the year in which I lost your mother, the year in which Raynald was born. It was on the 23rd of August. I was out on the mountains visiting some of my flock, about eight o'clock in the morning, when a most extraordinary water-spout was visible

in the heavens, over the Col Julian.
A perfect deluge was suspended in the
atmosphere; it hung there for a time like
a dark cloud of rain, and then broke suddenly over the peaks of the Col. The
inundation was fearful, like our Pelice,
when flooded with the melting snows of
spring. It went down both sides of the
mountain to the village of Pral, in St.
Martin, and down to Bobi, in our valley.
The people had hardly time to get out of
their houses before they were filled with
water, and swept away. Huge fragments
of rock were borne down by the stream,
crushing the houses, and killing many persons. The storm was awful; it came suddenly, and so it disappeared."

"But were you able to keep out of the
way, grandfather?" asked Valere.

"Yes, my boy, God preserved me. I
was out of danger, and able to pray
to God to succour those who were in
peril."

" Well, go on, grandfather, tell us again the history of the plague."

" In September, after this storm, there was a very extraordinary cold wind, which, as our friend Gilles has it, 'marched in company with a very dry haze.' It destroyed the fruit of those magnificent chestnuts with which our hills are covered, and under which, Etienne, you are so fond of playing, and picking up the fallen nuts."

" Yes, grandfather, but I always like to bring the best to you or Ardoine."

" Your mother first, my boy. Well, after the cold wind came a great quantity of rain, and this caused all our crop of grapes to perish. It seemed as if we were to suffer from a famine again, as we had done two years before, in 1628, when our people had such difficulty in living, as the priests had forbidden the Catholics to allow our brethren to work on their farms. We assembled together in synod on the 12th of September; our meeting was marked by great solemnity : a spirit of love drew us together, and knit us as one man. There were fifteen pastors; none thought that in a few months thirteen would have perished, and only two survive. It was in that year the convent and church of the Grey Friars at La Tour were built."

"What! that ugly-looking building," said Bertin, "that looks like a prison, and makes me tremble and run when I see the men inside the bars, with those things on their heads ?"

"Then we had, in 1630, the French army which Cardinal De Richelieu sent here, just as we have these French troops amongst us now under the Marshal Grancey. We were obliged to submit to France, as no help could be obtained; and I was one of those deputies who went to meet the king, Louis XIII., at the village of Montiers, not far from Lyons, to ask for the confirmation of our privileges. The plague had broken out in France, and was brought among us by the French. It appeared first at Les Portes in St. Germain and at Pral. As soon as it was known, we pastors met together at Pramol. Raynald took you there last summer, did he not?"

"Yes," said young Revel, who was all attention.

"That was where your grandfather stood twenty-five years ago, and you, Janavel, stood by my side. We met to seek the Lord, and by prayer, meditation, and conference to know the path of duty under our difficulties. We resolved to celebrate an extraordinary fast, but the armed men prevented our doing so; so each was to do what he could in his own parish. A few days after we had met at Pramol, the plague showed itself. We were then obliged to meet on the Sundays in the open fields; but as it was May, it caused us no discomfort."

"And was the plague then in our valley?"

"No, not yet; but it soon came to La Tour. The price of everything went up immensely; the French surgeon demanded fifty pistoles of gold for bleeding a man, and some persons gave away estates to friends, who would promise only to bury them if they died. On July the 12th, poor Bernardin, pastor of Pral, died, and on the 24th the pastor of Angrogna. Seven others died during the next month. The survivors met in that mountain which you all know, Mount Saumette, near the Vachère, and which is the nearest place to Angrogna, Pramol, and Prarusting. We met on the 2nd of August; there were only six of us then to do the work of all the churches. Three of the six died soon after."

"Oh, grandfather, and you were still alive, though you had seen so many others die!"

"Yes, God's providence preserved me. We three survivors met again on the heights of Angrogna, to consider what we could do to supply the churches. We wrote to Constantinople, to Geneva, and to Dauphiny. Not long after another died, and there remained only two to perform the duty for the whole of the three valleys."

"How many people do you think died, Etienne?" asked the Moderator.

"I have told you, I think, my boy."

"You said 12,000, grandfather."

"Yes, 12,000: at La Tour fifty families were swept away. The harvests rotted on the fields unreaped, the fruits dropped from the trees, horsemen fell from their horses in the middle of the road, and remained unburied on the spot—the great roads were strewn with so many bodies of men and beasts that it was dangerous to pass along them. The solitude of the desert came upon many towns; servants' wages were four times their ordinary rate, Lucille, and there were no nurses for the poor babies who were born at this time."

" Alas !" replied Martha, " I remember it well, and the difficulty I had in nursing Raynald."

" My friend and brother, Gilles, the historian, lost four of his sons. For some time I was alone, and had the care of all the churches. I went into all the parishes twice every Sunday, and once at least on every day in the week. I visited the sick without fear of death, knowing that the hairs of my head were numbered, and that a thousand might fall beside me, and ten thousand at my right hand, but it might not come nigh me. I passed amidst persons infected with the plague, and through villages which presented only spectacles of death, and I might truly say—

'Ubique,   .
Luctus, ubique pavor, et plurima mortis imago.'

It was at this time, when new pastors had come from Geneva, that we were obliged to use the French language for preaching instead of the Italian."

" And what more had you to do, grandfather, when the plague ceased ?"

"Oh, we had a great deal to do to
arrange matters in every parish, and it was
most extraordinary what a number of marriages took place afterwards. The reason
was plain—in most places the plague had
deprived husbands of their wives, and
wives of their husbands, so that each one
sought to be united again to some lone
sister or brother, in order to build up their
ruined houses. These marriages were not
celebrated with noise and mirth, as is common and natural, they were rather like the
conclusion of funeral solemnities; they
were marked by prayers to God, rather
than by the songs of the viol or tabret. We
suffered during that short period from the
three worst plagues that can afflict the
human race—famine, pestilence, and war,
but God's inscrutable providence preserved
me through that terrible time. I was one of
the two pastors who survived; but I feel now

that my time is **drawing near**; ere long I shall be gathered to my fathers, and perhaps in a way more dreadful than the visitation of the plague."

"Oh, don't say so, grandfather," said Etienne, "I am sure we cannot spare you; we should all miss you so much if you were to die."

"Well, children," said Janavel, "will you not thank grandfather for his interesting history? some of you will remember it, perhaps, after he has gone."

"Oh, yes," replied Valère, clapping his hands, "thank you, grandfather, your account is sad, but very interesting."

"I hope, please God," said Bertin, "that we shall have no plague in our days."

"We have the plague of monks," said Janavel, "and we cannot tell what evils they may bring about; but the same God who preserved my father through that stalking pestilence can preserve us. Children, see the sun is setting; say good bye to grandfather, for he is tired. You have arrived just in time, Raynald; take your hat, and escort the Moderator as far as the bridge of pines."

CHAPTER XVIII.

THE EDICT.

THE Moderator Léger was leaving La Baudène, and several of the family had assembled in the court to bid him farewell, and to watch the deepening shadows of evening, when they were startled by the tramp of approaching horses. They involuntarily turned their eyes in the direction of the sound, and observed, through the outer archway, a Piedmontese officer riding up the avenue which led to the farm. Passing through the half-opened door without ceremony, he advanced towards the group which was standing on the opposite side of the court.

He was dressed in the regimentals of Savoy; his spurred boots, his sword with its jewelled handle, his cap and plume, indicated him to be a person of distinction, and probably allied to noble blood. In his hand he carried a scroll of parchment, which he nervously unrolled and rolled several times.

"Heretics!" cried he, approaching the group, and holding out the scroll in his right hand, " your farm is outside the acknowledged limits in which you have been tolerated by law. Gastaldo, the Papal Delegate, has issued an order, commanding you to recant, and come to mass; if you will not, your lease is out in three days."

"Sir," said Janavel, "if this be indeed your commission, it may well cause us surprise and consternation. We have as yet heard nothing on the subject, and, without evidence, we hardly dare insult our Duke by supposing he could sanction so iniquitous a measure."

"The edict has his sanction," replied the officer. "He will have only Catholic tenants outside your guaranteed limits, and, in case of your refusal to comply with the terms, sends you notice to quit on the 28th."

"Oh, mother," said Susanne, "what does that strange man want, and what has he said, which makes grandfather look so unhappy?"

The gloom of sorrow was visible on the countenances of the group as they looked at the officer, and began to comprehend the purport of his mission.

Troubles which break in upon us unawares are often but gradually realized; after the first stupefaction and distrust, comes the poignancy of the bitter recoil, and then the event seems like some cruel dream, which has left us oppressed with a crushing weight, to understand which we must awake to reflection, and retrace the harrowing past.

It was thus with the family at La Baudène. The announcement of this edict fell upon them like a thunderbolt. Its first effect produced stupefaction and unbelief; its reaction horror and agony.

A silence, still as death, spell-bound that circle, during which the occasional champing of the horse's bit was the only sound audible. Raynald was the first to recover from the consternation of grief; he advanced towards the officer, and laying his hand on the bridle of the horse, said—

"By whose authority do you announce this order, and what have you to prove the truth of your assertion?"

"The proof of my commission is this parchment, signed by the Delegate Gastaldo, and sealed with the arms of Savoy. I bear the commission of the Duke, and am the son of the Marquis of Pianesse."

"The Duke," replied Raynald, bitterly, "might find more fitting work for his officers against his country's enemies, than sending them to bring misery into the peaceful families of his own subjects."

"You are Italians by birth," said Echard; "why do you not belong to the one true Church established in the land, and then you would be our brothers as well in creed as by blood?"

"Perhaps," said Raynald, "you are the officer in charge of these brigands and outlaws that come from Pignerol and elsewhere, to plunder and murder in our valleys."

"Call not the Duke's soldiers brigands, young man," retorted the officer, grasping his sword, "or it may fare badly with you unless you retract your words."

"And this is done in the name of religion!" continued Raynald. "What religion is this which makes us outcasts from our homes, and by threats of confiscation and death would win us to the Roman Church? Do you think Peter or Paul would have converted in this manner at Rome?"

" Keep your theology to yourself, young Luther. I am not sent here to argue, but to discharge my duty. You have heard your orders. If you want to keep your freeholds, you can see that an alternative is allowed you in the proclamation."

"Of base apostacy, I suppose," said Raynald; " for my part I would sooner forfeit every acre, than be seduced by the Pope of Rome or his monkish brigands."

" Young *barbet*, is this your submission to your Sovereign? I thought that loyalty was part of your creed."

" We have always been loyal," rejoined Rodolphe, " although the numerous outrages of this sort from which we have suffered have been enough to extinguish our allegiance to the house of Savoy."

" The edict is not mine, old man, I am but the bearer of it," said the officer, looking with interest at the group of children who were standing near the door. " It grieves me to serve this notice of ejectment, as you appear to be a large and happy family."

"Hypocrite," said Raynald, " add not insult to injury; we have heard so many soft professions from Rome's emissaries that we value them at their worth."

" Heretic dog," exclaimed the officer, "you will provoke me to do violence to my feelings to curb your insolence."

"I wish," continued Raynald, "that Gastaldo, or the Duke, had a month's experience of the mountains at this time of year."

"Hush, Raynald," said Rodolphe, approaching his grandson, "the Lord hath sent this young man, in his providence, even as He permitted Shimei to curse David. 'It is the Lord, let Him do what seemeth Him good.' Let not your temper embroil us, or it will be worse for us all."

" Aged father, your advice is sound," replied Echard, unrolling the parchment;

"to bend is easier than to resist, if you will not accept the terms. But I will read Gastaldo's edict, as I was ordered to publish it, and you will then see that I do not exceed my painful commission."

Echard then read in a loud and distinct voice the following :—

"André Gastaldo, Docteur ès Lois, Conseiller, Maitre Auditeur ordinaire, seant en la très-Illustre Chambre des Comtes de S. A. R. et Conservateur general de la Sainte Foy, pour l'observation des Ordres publiés contre la pretenduë Religion Reformée des Vallées de Lucerne, de Perouse, et de S. Martin, et à cet effet specialement deputé par S. A. R."

After mumbling rapidly to himself the beginning of the order, he continued in a loud tone :—

"Qu'ils ayent, dans trois jours prochains, depuis la publication et execution

ECHARD ANNOUNCING GASTALDO'S EDICT.

Page 220.

des presentes, à se retirer, abandonner, et delaisser les dits lieux avec toutes leurs familles, et se transporter és quartiers et limites que S. A. R. tolere, jusqu' à son bon plaisir, qui sont Bobbi, Villar, Angrogne Roras, et la contrée des Bonnets, sous peine de la vie, et de la confiscation de leurs maisons et biens, qui se rencontrent hors des dites limites : *et ce toutes-fois et quantes que dans vingt jours suivans, ils ne facent conster par devant nous qu'ils se sont Catholisés, ou qu'ils ont vendu leurs biens à des Catholiques.*

"Donné à Lucerne le 25 Janvier, 1655.

"Signé :

"ANDRÉ GASTALDO,

"Auditeur Deputé."

" Friend," said Janavel, looking the officer steadily in the face, " tell your Duke not to play the hypocrite before the world by saying that he punishes us for rebellion, and not for our religion. We have always been loyal, and have served him well in different times of need. Our obedience to this cruel edict will prove that we are loyal. It is only for our religion that he persecutes us. You see that all is conceded if we will abjure and go to mass."

"Well, you must settle that with the Duke, or Gastaldo; I am not responsible for their deeds nor motives. I have only to tell you a plain fact, although it's a sad one; and an irritating one as would appear from the temper of my friend there, who seemed inclined to try his strength with me; but I presume I should be a match for his long arms, or I am mistaken."

"The Pope's officers always take good care to keep their steel gloves on when there's danger," retorted Raynald. "Throw away your jewelled sword, and I should not be afraid to try your sinews, and see if the pampered courtier would match the peasant who has fed on pulse and water."

" Low-born churl," said Echard, losing his temper, " since you are so anxious for the experiment the opportunity may come hereafter."

"Oh, sir," said Martha, clasping his knee, and looking up into his face with a look of unutterable emotion, which thrilled Echard to his soul, " have mercy on us! look at that old man, my father; is there no regard due to those white hairs? how can he survive if turned out in the snow and rain upon the mountains at this time of the year? Look at our little ones— will you scatter us? will you kill us? Oh, be our friend—intercede for us."

" Madam," said Echard, overcome with the earnest appeal, " I grieve for you. God forgive me if I am instrumentally a destroyer of homes, and a scatterer of the fatherless. I can almost feel myself that there is something in your glorious Alps which makes you love your free mountain home."

Echard felt the searching eloquence of those tearful eyes, gazing upon him with an intensity of eagerness, as if a thousand throbbing memories struggled within her breast. At length, overcome with her feelings, Martha fainted and sank into Raynald's arms.

Echard strove to conceal his emotion, and turned his eyes on Janavel, whose quiet dignity and noble mien, bearing the stamp of nature's nobility, elicited his admiration.

He gazed for a moment at the women and the surrounding children, whose voices were hushed from instinctive sympathy with their parents' grief. He remembered the rumours that he had heard of this peculiar family, and the thought that Iolande was probably their guest increased his interest.

" Sir," said Janavel, interrupting his reflections, and addressing him as he was turning his horse to depart, " your coun-

tenance declares that your heart is not yet
seared with hypocrisy and blood. Would
that the Duke would reconsider his edict!
Look round at our home which you will
break up ; your courage, I doubt not, would
lead you in the front of the battle, but act
not towards us as if we were enemies. If
you tremble in the discharge of this present commission, it will do honour to your
heart as a man, and to your courage as a
soldier."

"I feel your words, but I cannot help
you. I now bid you good-day, for I must
call on your neighbours ; you had better be
packing up your moveables, while there is
time, for the Irish and the French may be
coming along the road, and a starving
hawk will not fatten nor last long on what
they leave."

"Alas !" said Echard to himself as he
rode away. " Is this the fruit of religion?
To outrage persons because they are of a
different creed, to oppress loyal subjects,

to make the widow and fatherless homeless in the midst of winter? My conscience is in doubt; I do not altogether
approve of these deeds, although I am a
Catholic, and have heard the arguments
by which these actions are vindicated. I
cannot help feeling that this edict is harsh
and unjust, and my feelings revolt against
the employment of force or cruelty to win
converts to our creed. If our Church be
true, and they are really in danger of hell
fire, as our monks keep telling us, it seems
to me we ought to try the effect of kindness and persuasion in this world, for
they will have to suffer enough hereafter.
It is a commission I do not relish, and
no honour to a soldier either. After all
I have much less zeal and faith since I have
been to Rome, and know what takes place
behind the scenes.

"Methinks this seems a loving family.
I like the bold spirit of that young fellow,
who was inclined to skirmish with me,

and the calm intrepid glance of his father's
eagle eye. O Lord! lay not this sin to
the charge of the unwilling instrument."

Indulging in these reflections, Echard
galloped up the valley, until he reached
Les Eyrals at the entrance of La Tour.

CHAPTER XIX.

"THIS edict is most unjust and cruel!" exclaimed Raynald with indignation, as the family gathered together the next evening to arrange their plans.

"My boy," said Rodolphe, "there are too many precedents for it in history, and Rome boasts of being *semper eadem*. It is what Castrocaro did when he was governor of the valleys nearly a hundred years ago, in 1566, when he commanded our fathers to quit their dwellings in twenty-four hours, under the pain of confiscation and death; then, in 1601, I remember, when I was a young man, an order was published in the

Marquisate of Saluces, requiring our
brethren to go to mass, or to leave under
the same penalties. And some of you, my
children, may recollect, in 1634, how the
Prefect Ressan drove our friends out of
the commune of Campillon in twenty-four
hours, in the execution of a similar order.
It reminds me of the passage in Virgil I
was reading to you, Raynald—

      " ' Veteres migrate coloni,
Nunc victi, tristes, quoniam fors omnia versat.' "

"But the edict is unjust as well as
cruel—is it not, grandfather?"

"Yes, our right to live here, if not to
preach, has been recognized by numerous
edicts, as in the noted one of 1561. Again,
in 1603, we paid six thousand ducats for
the right of habitation, and the confirmation of all our past privileges; and it was
only last November that our Moderator
submitted to Gastaldo, and to the Counts
Ressan and Christopel, the originals of our

conceded privileges, which were admitted
as valid, and were confirmed again by his
Royal Highness."

" What are the motives, then, which
induce the Duke to forget the past, and
change his conduct so soon ?"

" They are, doubtless, many and com-
plicated," said Janavel.   " I attribute most
to the jubilee of 1650, with its first-fruits,
the institution of the Propaganda at Turin ;
then advantage is taken of the settlement
of monks in every commune, of the cantonment of soldiers, and of the various calum-
nies which have been so artfully spread
against us."

" But, children," said Rodolphe, " let
us consider our plans and decide our movements ; for, though the edict speaks of an
alternative, I think we are all of one mind,
and ready to suffer rather than——"

" Recant," interrupted Janavel.   " Indeed we are.   Our loyalty to the Duke is
unquestioned in matters civil ; but where

liberty of conscience is concerned, we must obey God rather than man."

"But it's hard to bear what is so shamefully unjust," said Raynald, his eye flashing with indignation. "The Duke ought to remember our services in '38, '39, and '40. I've often heard you speak of our loyalty when the Princes Maurice and Thomas excited a revolution in Piedmont, so that Madame was obliged to fly from Turin."

"True," replied Janavel, "we did not swerve from our allegiance to the throne. Our valley of Lucerna was especially loyal, and was in consequence cruelly ravaged by the Marquis of Angrogna, who was in open revolt."

"And this edict is our reward for loyalty, because we are Protestants! while the great rebellion of the Catholics is easily forgotten."

"Well, Raynald," calmly rejoined Rodolphe, "let us discern the finger of God, who turneth the hearts of men as rivers of water, and who maketh the wicked the ministers of his purpose. May his presence go with us, and give us rest; with Him we have all things, and Paul counted all things but loss for the excellency of Christ. The old saying is quite true—

"'Sine summo bono, nihil bonum.'"

"What plan would you suggest, father?" asked Janavel. "I thought we might move to Villar, where our friends Jahier and Michelin would afford us shelter, and there await the course of events. It is one of the four places mentioned in the edict, and within our immemorial limits."

"I am afraid," suggested Madeleine in a choking voice, "that the soldiers who are quartered there will molest us."

"Should there be any danger of that, Janavel, it would be wiser for us to separate, and move to the higher valleys. Some of us might find shelter in Angrogna, others at Rora, and *in extremis* we must, like our ancestors, take refuge in the caverns of Castelluzzo; but these are casualties which I trust may not happen."

"What do you think, father, we should do with our guest, Iolande; would it not be safer for her to leave us?"

"Oh, do not desert me, kind protectors, I wish to learn more of your faith, which seems so much better than ours. I cannot leave Ardoine, for whom I now feel the love of a sister."

"What arrangements have you made about sister Marie?" whispered Martha to her husband.

"We must fetch a litter from La Tour, and transport her up the valley to Villar."

"I fear," said Marguerite, "she will not stand the exposure, especially at this time of the year."

"Alas!" replied Janavel, "there is no help; to leave her here longer than is necessary is to expose her to danger. And we should not forgive ourselves if anything happened to her. Raynald," continued he, "have you spoken about parting with our farm? Does not the edict give us the option of selling it, or are we to be beggared by that legal robbery called confiscation?"

"To be obliged to sell, father, within a given time is like giving away a thing. People won't buy when they know you must sell, but will rather wait for the chapter of accidents."

"Oh, it is a grievous thing," interrupted Lucille. "My home, my home, alas! how can I leave it?"

"I suppose," said Janavel, "our lands will be given to the Catholics who eject us. I heard to-day that there are a number of Irishmen in the country, and that the Duke thinks of settling them here."

"If this be so," replied Daniel, "we must do the best we can before it is too late. Raynald, you were to speak to our neighbour Manchon, and see if you could come to terms about the land. This land adjoins his, and would be a valuable addition to his property."

"So I did; but he's like all the rest, full of professions when there's no danger of a test, but full of difficulties when the opportunity arises."

"That is odd," said Janavel, "for it has been the staple of his conversation since I was a boy. When he could for a moment cease talking about himself, he declared he envied this plot of ground, which would just fill up the irregular shape of his farm, and make it a 'unity,' as he called it."

"He was willing to bargain, but his terms were so low that they were an insult. It is really iniquitous to eject us from our lawful property, and then virtually to rob us of it, so that we are sent forth like beggars."

"Hush, my boy," said Jean, "let us

not arraign God's providences. He sees
the end from the beginning, which we do
not. We must trust and look to Him, and
not to second causes. When we look at
them we feel a natural irritation. But
our minds only get composed by looking
above the instrument to the real Mover,
and feeling that He has his wise purposes."

"Right, brother," said Janavel, "that
is what Paul would have done, and what
the Christians of old time did when there
was less wealth and more faith in the
Church. Iolande, you shall go with us. I
trust you will learn more of our creed, that
you may be able to join our communion.
Our morality is not expediency, so you
may rest on our words as on a sister's
oath, and feel that your life and honour
shall be safe in our keeping."

"Ah, here comes Barba Léger," said
Valère, hastening to meet the Moderator.
"We are so sad, Barba."

"I know you are, my boy. Good day,

Father Rodolphe, I doubt not your heart is fixed, trusting in the Lord."

"I hope it is," replied the patriarch. "Paul would count even this a light affliction, which is but for a moment in contrast with the eternal weight of glory. You have done well, Moderator, in coming; I thought your kind heart would prompt you to sympathize with us."

"Weep with them that weep," replied the pastor. "I shall soothe you more not by attempting to staunch your tears, but rather by mingling mine with them."

"How can we better consecrate our last moments," said Rodolphe, "than by the commemoration of our Saviour's dying love? Raynald, you have long been preparing yourself for this holy feast; let us renew, then, for the last time, our family sacrifice of praise and thanksgiving. Ardoine?—where's the child?"

"She went to Aunt Marie a few minutes ago," said Raynald.

"Then in half an hour you can join them, and prepare them for our coming, if Marie feels equal to the exertion. 'We will take the cup of salvation, and call upon the name of the Lord.'"

CHAPTER XX.

MOTHER AND DAUGHTER.

"Mother, dear mother," said Ardoine, bending over the invalid, and moistening her lips with fresh water, "you look so tired, I hope you do not feel worse; there, that will refresh you; stay, let me add a drop of lemon juice, and that will give it more flavour."

"Thanks, daughter," said Marie, with difficulty; "you see how frail my life is, I may leave you at any moment."

"Oh, don't say so, mother, the world would become a blank to me if you were taken away; everything would lose its in-

terest; I am very, very happy with my
aunts; but you are a mother, and a mother
is nature's friend, and is only given to us
once in our lives. You are all the world
to me, although you are a prisoner in your
sick bed."

"But suppose that I should be taken
from you, Ardoine; I should like to feel
that I left you in some one's safe keeping,
it would make me die happier."

"Oh, mother, what makes you talk like
this? It makes my heart heavy. I trust
God will spare you to us for some time
yet; but don't be unhappy about me, for
I am sure you might leave me safely in
Uncle Janavel's charge, you know how
kind and fatherly he is."

"I am sure he will be a father to you;
but you are now grown up, and it is not
unlikely that the thought of marriage may
have crossed your mind."

"Marriage!" artlessly replied Ardoine,
"I do not think it has; I have been so

happy with you, that I have not thought
on the subject."

"Is there no one among your friends,"
whispered the invalid, "for whom you feel
any attachment?"

"Not in the sense you mean. You
know you have taught me to look upon
marriage in a serious light, and as I have
not associated with the Catholic girls on
the neighbouring farm I have heard little
on this subject."

"Then tell me, my daughter, how should
you like Raynald? you know he is a great
favourite of mine; he would be kind to
you, and you have known each other's characters from youth."

"Oh, mother, poor dear Raynald, I
do love him; but he's like my brother, and
I never thought about marrying him."
She paused as the conversation of the
day before floated across her mind in a new
light.

"But you can think of it now that I

have suggested the thought—consider he
is a good young man, and has the fear of
God in his heart, and I think loves you.
You must have guessed that before now.
Women they say are quick-witted enough
in some things."

"Then I am duller, I fear, than my sex
generally. I know Raynald likes my company, and we have always been the best of
friends ; but, indeed, the idea of marriage
is new, for I have never thought of him in
that light."

"But you have a regard for him, and
that may deepen into a warmer attachment."

"Oh, dear mother, don't press me.
You know how I love you, and how I
would do anything to make you happy.
You cannot force the heart, and I have
heard you say yourself, when talking of
early days, that we need a dash of romance
to help us through the routine of after life,
and especially when we become acquainted

with the foibles of each other's character."

"Daughter, I may die at any moment, and to see you married to one who would appreciate your worth, would have been a comfort to me in my last moments. You have had a bright example of domestic bliss in our present home. We were six sisters, and we married six brothers, and I may truly add, not from *convenance* but from love; do you not think so, judging by results?"

"Indeed I do, mother, our home has been like a little paradise; we have been very happy."

"Alas!" replied Marie, "Raynald has been in to me this morning with very sad news, and this makes me more anxious to speak to you on the subject of marriage. The Duke has issued an edict commanding us to become Roman Catholics and go to mass, or to leave our farm in three days."

"But surely, mother, he does not really mean to put it into execution."

"I fear he does. You know how often these things have chequered our history. Oh, think of our beloved home being taken from us, and our becoming outcasts in our valleys."

"Dearest mother, what will become of you? I am young and strong, and can work for our living, if some of our friends in the higher valleys will receive us. But how could you travel?"

"Think not of me, dear child, I hover on the brink of eternity. I am approaching, step by step, the stream of death, that river Jordan, but my Saviour whispers to me, 'Let not your heart be troubled, for I, who was lifted up on Calvary's cross, will never forsake thee.' Oh, my daughter, was there ever love like this? How transporting the thought of spending a glorious eternity with such a God of purity and love, to go no more out, but to worship in his holy temple for ever. I shall soon reach my home, for I feel that I shall not outlive these scenes, and it will be well that I should not. My trust in the death and merits of Christ is unclouded, and my departure is a source of joy. I mourn only for the troubles which must attend those I leave behind, and I feel most anxious that you should have a natural protector."

"Oh, mother, how I love my home, it will be terrible to be turned out; and what shall I do if you also should be taken from me?"

"You see, my daughter, there is an urgent reason why I should plead for Raynald. Is it not right that you should have a protector in these troublous times? And can you find one so devoted, so good, so brave? Let your mother's dying voice plead for him, and tell you what his modesty and fear will not allow him to say himself."

"Mother, mother," said Ardoine, sobbing, "this is very painful. Love cannot be forced, and you would not like to make me pledge myself to what I might possibly regret hereafter. Dear Raynald is indeed good, and I love him as a brother; but I could not in a moment change my habit of feeling towards him, and regard him in the relationship you suggest."

"True, my daughter, true. Will you go so far as to promise me that you will not marry without the approbation of Pastor Léger, our Moderator, and Uncle Janavel. Promise me this before I die."

"This I can readily do, because they would not oppose anything that was for my real welfare."

"Promise me, moreover, that you will never wed a Roman Catholic."

"Mother, what makes you allude to such things? or why should you ask me this question? I trust you have never seen anything in me to make it necessary to bind me; but on this point, of course, I can most readily assure you. So I trust you will now feel happy. I must pray to God to direct me in this most important step, and also to help us all through the trials which appear to be coming upon us. May God preserve you long to us, dear mother," added Ardoine, as she stooped down and kissed her death-like face.

"Fear not, my daughter; how often does the storm burst upon us with a blessing, and Christ comes to us when we least expect Him. When you find me dead, do not look at my poor body, but think that I am with my God, praising Him in all the realization of that which I now believe."

A tap was heard at the door, and Raynald entered. Treading lightly lest he should disturb his aunt, he approached her bed.

"The Moderator is here, dear aunt, and grandfather is anxious for us all to join you in celebrating the Holy Supper, if you feel well enough."

"Oh, yes, always well enough to commemorate my Saviour's love, which passeth knowledge."

CHAPTER XXI.

THE FIRST COMMUNION.

A SOLEMN stillness pervaded Marie's chamber, although a large group knelt around her bed, and many of the younger children were present.

The hoary-headed Rodolphe, sinking from the decay of nature; Marie, prostrate with disease; Raynald, the athletic mountaineer, full of buoyant health; Ardoine, the type of youth and beauty; the sorrowing Martha, clad in her habitual mourning; the little Lena, tottering to the foot of the bed, and steadying herself by grasping the coverlid, formed a suggestive group full of typical contrasts.

Since the announcement of Gastaldo's edict, every member of the household had been more assiduous at the sick bed, and had looked upon Marie with increased tenderness, as if from an undefined misgiving that her time was short, and from apprehensions of the gloomy future.

Marie herself, who might naturally have mourned most grievously under this cruel blow, maintained her usual serenity. Her soul seemed more than ever emancipated from the body. The God of hope filled her with joy and peace in believing, so that she abounded in hope, through the power of the Holy Ghost. Hope, glorious hope! that outleaps the present and lays the dim future under preliminary tribute; hope, less abstract than faith, because instinct with more personality, invigorated her soul while striving to explore the undiscovered glories of heaven, which dilated with greater vividness from contrast with the bitter present.

The hearts of that silent band were

burning within them, for their present distress gave intensity to their prayers, as
they secretly supplicated grace for one
another in the approaching hour of trial.

It was Raynald's first communion; it
will be his last in the home of his fathers.
He had of late become more established in
his ancestral faith, though previously his
religious impressions had ebbed and flowed,
increasing in depth when he left the association of home, and waxing fainter by a
strange contradiction when he returned.

He had for some time been anxious to
solemnize his good resolutions by joining
in this holy feast with his aunt, to whom
he felt deeply indebted for encouragement
and instruction; while Marie, on her part,
looked on him with peculiar affection, from
the hope that she had advanced his spiritual
interests.

Raynald was earnest and sincere, though
occasionally betrayed by his impulsive temper; yet he was patient of rebuke, and

ready to acknowledge an error when self-convicted. He had much to learn of those passive graces which are the glory of the gospel; but his heart was upright, he endeavoured to act up to his knowledge of truth, and was greatly influenced by the consistency of Ardoine's example. His religious feeling was the only alleviation to his mother's sorrow, and her heart would rally when her son prayed with her, and when she listened to his earnest tone, at the bedside of his afflicted aunt.

After the accustomed prayers, the pastor Léger approached Marie, and gave her the broken bread. The cup trembled as he held it to her lips, and the words of administration fell solemnly on the ears of all. Ardoine communicated after her mother. Giving the cup to Raynald, who knelt by her side, the Moderator placed his right hand on the young man's head, and breathed a prayer for his establishment in the faith.

"Father and pastor," whispered Marie,

when the ceremony was concluded, "our impending trial seems like a dream, but as regards myself, the prospect of death is one of joy and not of sorrow; for I am now ready to be offered up, and the time of my departure is at hand."

"I rejoice," said the Moderator, "that you can still triumph over death."

"I can embrace death as a messenger of peace. 'The sting of death is sin; but thanks be to God, who giveth us the victory through our Lord Jesus Christ.'"

"You can rest confidently," said Rodolphe, "on Christ's finished work on the cross."

"I can, father. Christ did not do his work by halves. He has flung the door of heaven wide open for us by his death, and sits there at all hours; for, thanks be to God, there is no unseasonable faith."

"To what would you compare the love of Christ?" asked Raynald.

"It is not to be compared to anything;

it is boundless and unfathomable. I would not lose what I feel for ten thousand worlds. My heart overflows with love. Eternity is full of it; heaven and earth are full; Christ is full; it is an inexhaustible fountain."

"You do not rest on your own merits or good works?" said the pastor.

"God forbid; I am a sinner, redeemed solely by the blood of Jesus. Sin is the abhorrence of my soul; it is a burden too heavy for me to bear, and yet daily do I see more of my indwelling sin."

"And yet you are not afraid to die," said Martha.

"No, indeed! It is not dying; my soul shall soar on wings of love to my Saviour. The body will moulder in the earth, and ripen for glory. It is now like a fetter and clog to my spirit, which longs to be above."

"What makes you feel so sure that you are God's?" asked Raynald.

"The witness of his Spirit. I pray that his Holy Spirit may dwell in me, and momentarily free me from all my sins, from those that nature cannot discover."

"Can you feel heaven within you?"

"I have a foretaste of joy that it is impossible to describe. I often spend the whole night in communion with my God, and find it far too short. I pray that Father, Son, and Holy Spirit may all come down and dwell in me, and that they may enlarge my heart to receive them."

"Pastor," continued Marie, after a pause, "in this solemn hour, when exile or death seems before us, let me, in the presence of my loved ones, commit my daughter to your care as well as to theirs. She will recognize you as a father, for you have sweetened her mother's years of pain, and have been her own instructor from childhood. Moderator, will you, with Janavel, be guardian to my child, and advise her in the perplexities of life?"

" Daughter," replied Léger, " she is already dear to me as one of my own flock, but will become doubly dear when commended to me by your dying breath."

" Mother," said Ardoine, " I accept him as my father ; commit your orphan to God, and fear not for me ; I am persuaded that we shall meet around the throne of God in heaven."

" The peace of God," said Léger, rising to depart, "keep your hearts, and after that ye have suffered a while, bring each one of you unto his eternal glory, through Christ Jesus. Amen."

Shortly afterwards Raynald came forth alone from his aunt's chamber. He did not repeat the subject of their conversation even to his mother, but his downcast look and tearful eye were proofs that the strong man's heart had been bowed by disappointment and grief. For some time he trembled when he saw Ardoine, as if he dreaded the exchange of glances. But his various duties to his family in this time of trial afforded relief to his mind; while with undiminished affection he still watched Ardoine's every look and anticipated her wishes, soothing himself with the hope that his devotion might gradually change her sisterly love into one of a more absorbing character.

CHAPTER XXII.

THE LAST TIME.

THE last time! It is a sentence with which all are familiar, but whose sad pathos is unacknowledged until drafted into real life. It is an experience which most of us have felt; it is one which all must some time feel.

The last time! It is a wail of sorrow, of sorrow which melts indifferent souls together, having made them feel that they cannot stand alone; of sorrow bitter as the dirge over the tomb of the loved and lost. It is a plaint of memory as well as of the heart. Memory, kindly faithless to the bitter, and more kindly faithful to the pleasant, recalls the past with a softened yet melancholy enchantment, and in its lenient retrospects forms a more irksome contrast with the galling present. The ills over which we once wept seem trivial now that they have receded, and bygone pleasures seem doubly sweet in the mellowings of the past.

The last time! A change is at hand. The heart throbs from the consciousness of an undefined void; for we cling to what we know, we tremble before the untried.

Ye heartless, who boast of your insensibility, know that Nature brands you as traitors to herself. A heart is Nature's priceless gift; emotion is mental, moral, and spiritual life; and when sin is removed our souls will then feel intense and complex pleasures for evermore, . and renew their strength with the buoyancy of eternal bliss. Feeling is the essence of all pleasures, happiness is their sum. That we do not feel is our shame and curse.

The loving family, united in their home to-day, from which to-morrow they will be exiles; the sisters circling round the youths, who are quitting their country for a foreign clime; the maiden, folded in the arms of him whom duty summons to the stormy ocean; the father clasping his only son on the eve of the battle; the mother dropping tears on her first-born babe, ere the coffin shrouds her bright idol for ever; the wife embracing her husband in the cell of the condemned;—these have their deep, yet varied experiences of the same short, simple, heart-stirring words — "the last time!"

That patriarchal family weep upon their own threshold; the fatal day approaches when they must leave, and seek the mountain glen, the lonely forest, or the dripping cavern. Earth must be their home, nature their friend, the heavens their covering. Their place shall know them no more.

Alas! in those words "no more" there lurks a volume of mystic dread, and the soul shudders under that emphasis of grief.

Feelings like these were experienced at this time, not by units, but by hundreds, as they have been at other times by thousands, through the cruelty of the apostate Church of Rome. In this family we contemplate one solitary type.

* * * * * *

The sensitive Madeleine felt as only a wife and mother could feel, the bitterness of the exile and the pang of the homeless; and she wandered over every nook and corner of the house, weeping bitterly. She had had her experiences of suffering; she had bent over her husband's corpse, and had felt the crowding memories of grief and the crowding griefs of memory. She had looked upon that countenance which she had loved, at the eyes which once met hers with smiles, at the closed lips whose voice

was music, and had felt the poignancy
of those words, "the last time!" Her
riven heart bled afresh at the prospect
of being torn from her home, that last link
with her beloved husband. Each spot
awakened plaintive memories; each room
revived experiences of praise or prayer,
sorrow or joy; each stone had been trodden
by the children's feet; this or that place
recalled some special loved one, but the
home itself recalled them all.

* * * * * *

A solemnity, as of an approaching
death, reigned through the family circle of
La Baudène on the evening of the 27th of
January, and even the prattle of the little
ones was hushed. Some, blissfully unconscious of the morrow, had sought their
mother's couch, as they had done all their
lives, and supposed they should do for the
future. They were wrapt in that sweet
sleep which is the birthright of childhood,
and the envy of old age; but some of the

elder boys and girls remained up later than usual, and their silence was in accord with their parents' sorrow.

"Children," said the aged Rodolphe, speaking in a tremulous tone, "never did I expect to bid you farewell upon our own hearth. I thought that under this roof my daughters would have surrounded my dying bed, and closed my eyes. Children, sorrows which the young deem trivial weigh heavily on the aged. How much, then, must I feel this crushing blow? I have been here fourscore years and more. This home is dear to me, for you were born here, your children have been born here, and you can feel, as parents, the sacred interest with which this invests the place. Daughters, I am an old man; my grey hairs are not suited for the mountain blast, nor my feeble steps to cross the gorge; leave me here to die, for if it be the Lord's will I shall soon enter into my rest."

"Father," said Martha, "my husband

is your son; we will cherish you so long as God spares us to one another."

"I know, my daughters, your filial affection; your love to each other hath been singular, uniting you in one unbroken household. Our memories may well be sad when the past has been so bright, for few have had our happy experiences of domestic life."

"Few, indeed, father," said Janavel. "Our home has been holy ground, but we must hope to find another asylum in our beloved valleys. Their very stones are dear to us, and we would rather lodge in our mountain caverns than in the palaces of Rome."

"Come, dear grandfather," said Ardoine, "you have eaten nothing to-night; let me prepare your evening meal as usual, although, alas! I could weep when I feel your words, that it is for the last time."

"My daughters, try and follow the dear child's advice. Eat bread, for this is good for you. Nature must be supported even in her griefs."

"Oh, my father, it is heart-rending to think that we shall never again meet in this way, never again see you in your accustomed place. Oh, save us from the morrow! Your New Year's warning, that we knew not what the year might bring forth, is sadly realized."

"My children, look to the Lord, for He only can support."

At this moment the broken cough of Marie was heard, and it recalled their attention to the absent sister.

"Ah! poor Marie," said Madeleine, "how will she bear it? Is it true that this is her last night here, after her long confinement of twenty-one years?"

"It is a sad thought," murmured Rodolphe, "that the charity of the Romish Church will cast her out homeless and houseless. Children, let us turn to God. Ardoine, give me my Bible. Now, my child, open it for me at Hebrews xiii. 'Here we have no continuing city, but seek one to come.' We now feel this to be true, because we enter into its sad experience. And then look at that eleventh chapter, how full it is of bright examples of faith! Consider Abraham; it was no slight test to bid him sell all that he had, and go as a stranger into a land of which he knew not. Our test is the same."

" May the Lord grant us grace to stand the refining process," said David, " and to endure the spoiling of our goods, rather than do violence to our conscience."

" God grant it," replied Janavel. "To quit our homes, and go forth destitute, for conscience' sake, is a moral spectacle; it is a triumph of faith, and can only be done through the help of God's Holy Spirit."

" My children, I trust that none of our people will recant through fear of suffering, and join the apostates. Let us endure as

seeing Him who is invisible, for at the last
we shall reap if we faint not."

"You know, dear grandfather, that
beautiful verse you taught me, 'Be thou
faithful unto death, and I will give thee a
crown of life.'"

"Yes, let us try to imitate our fore-
fathers, whose memories and faith we
cherish. These dear old valleys, that we
love so much, have seen them in their
hours of trial; and we must not cause
those snows to blush, should they see us
flinching from the same path. All things
pass away; we shall soon be gone. But
our valleys will still remain to preach to
our sons. May they remind them of our
patience and faith, as well as of our sufferings! May our memories be graven on our
rocks, for the righteous shall be had in
everlasting remembrance!"

"Father," said Marguerite, "won't
you read and pray with us to-night as
usual? We must not neglect to do what

we have ever done, especially when it is for the last time."

"Yes, my children, let us sing our evening hymn, according to our custom. I know it may be almost a painful effort; but try, Renée. Let us sing in the name of Jesus, and seek his presence."

"I will do my best, but my sisters will pardon me if I falter."

The band of exiles then stood up, and chanted the ninetieth Psalm.

"Lord, Thou hast been our dwelling-place in all generations.

"Before the mountains were brought forth, or ever Thou hadst formed the earth and the world, even from everlasting to everlasting, Thou art God.

"For all our days are passed away in Thy wrath: we spend our years as a tale that is told.

"So teach us to number our days, that we may apply our hearts unto wisdom.

" Return, O Lord, how long ? and let it repent Thee concerning Thy servants.

" Oh satisfy us early with Thy mercy, that we may rejoice and be glad all our days.

" Make us glad according to the days wherein Thou hast afflicted us, and the years wherein we have seen evil."

The old man closed his Bible, and his sons and daughters knelt round him, while he implored Divine guidance and support.

" God of our fathers," said he; " God of Abraham, Isaac, and Jacob, look upon us in our distress, for Christ's sake. O Thou who didst suffer for our sins, and dost know what human suffering is, for Thou didst feel it to a degree we never can conceive, look upon us, and be merciful; be our God in our wanderings, as Thou wast Jacob's; defend us, and after the changes of this life bring us all to thine everlasting kingdom, to be part of Christ's elect, of whom the whole family in heaven and earth is named. Then may our family meet around the throne, not for the last time, but for ever. We shall sing eternal praises to our Redeemer, and remember no more the trials of this life, for they will not be worthy to be compared with the glory which shall be revealed. God give us his Holy Spirit, and grant our requests for Jesus Christ's sake."

The twin sisters, after their father's bene-diction, returned to Madeleine's chamber. They stood for some time motionless, as if gazing at some object which entranced them both. They were looking into a cradle where two infants, a boy and a girl, slept, folded in each other's arms. One was Marguerite's, the other Madeleine's. The mothers looked in silence, for the joy with which they had long beheld those infants was now merged in sorrow. The children, who were in the bloom of health, slept soundly and peacefully. The glossy curls of the little Aline lay on the boy's face, and her half-opened hand unconsciously rested on his neck. The mothers looked at the pair, each, doubtless, thinking most of her own. They stood with their arms entwined, and Madeleine's head leaning on Marguerite's shoulder. Just then Aline was seen to smile in her sleep, as if she had heard an angel whisper; and the mothers themselves could hardly refrain from a tearful smile when they saw this little one so unconscious of the morrow, slumbering in the sweet recklessness of innocence and in the repose of childhood's faith.

"May the Lord watch over our babes, if their poor mothers cannot!" said Marguerite. "We know not what may happen, as father said at the beginning of the year. We could not tell what it had in store for us, and January has set gloomily enough upon us; has it not?"

"Alas! it has," replied Madeleine, "and I feel a sad forecast of doubt and fear, as if this were only the beginning of troubles. Oh! Marguerite, a horrible dread oppresses me," continued she, bursting into tears, and throwing her arms around her sister's neck. "Leave me not, I implore you. Oh! sister, sister, I cannot leave you, and the dear house, and the children."

"Hush, dearest; look, your grief hath half-awakened our little ones. Hush! let us pray for strength to bear what it has pleased God to lay upon us. There now, wipe your eyes, and promise you will try to support me. Let us do what we can to comfort our dear ones, and to cheer father, for this is our duty under present circum- stances. Come, Madeleine, take one more look at our sleeping babes, and then we must retire to rest."

"Oh! sister, is it for the last time in this dear home of our fathers? Sleep on, sweet babes! may you never know the bitterness of heart which your mothers feel!" As she said this she stooped over the cradle to kiss them, while her tears fell on their little faces. The precious drops (sad memorials of a mother's heart and of individual grief) trickling slowly downwards, glistened for a short time upon the infants' cheeks, and then dried up; but they had been seen in heaven.

CHAPTER XXIII.

GASTALDO.

THE twenty-eighth of January dawned upon the Valley of Lucerna, and kindled in many a heart far different emotions to those which New Year's day had excited but a few weeks before.

Nature ushered it in with unwonted gloom — sullen and drenching clouds brooded over the valleys, swathing even the base of the Vandalin, while the heights of La Vachère, Friouland, and Bagnol were all hidden in an impenetrable sea of mist.

" Oh ! mother," exclaimed Etienne, as he caught hold of her apron, " what are

my aunts doing ? Everything is upset, as
if we were moving to the high Alps. It's
not the time yet for going to the châlets
with our cows, that's in summer ; look at
the rain and fog, the snow has been falling
in the night, all the roofs are quite white,
and it's my birthday, and I always spend
it at home."

"Little one," said Martha, as she
caressed the boy, "cruel men have come
to turn us out of our home. I hope we
shall find another at Villar, with pastor
Léger's friends. You went up there once,
you may remember, when you had such a
happy day, and were loth to come back."

"Yes," said the child, "but that was
in the summer, it was then warm and
bright, now there is no sun, and the snow
is so cold, and it rains so fast. Is it the
Duke who is sending us away in this
weather ?"

" I don't think he would turn us out,"
said Martha, "for he knows that we are

loyal servants, but he is surrounded by those who advise him to act' in this way, and so we must obey."

"And are you going away to-day? Must I leave my playthings behind? Shall not I be able to run any more under the old mulberry tree, nor to play with sissy in the meadow?" And the little boy sobbed aloud.

"Come, Etienne," said his mother, kissing him, "come, I will tell you what grandfather was talking about last night. He said that 'here we have no continuing city, but seek one to come.' Don't you remember what Ardy told you when little Malan died last year?"

"Yes, Ardy told me death was a journey to another world, that she had gone where God lives, that we were all travelling the same way, and none can tell how long we may remain on earth."

"Good child to remember so well. It will not be so sad to move up the valley as to see a friend laid in the cold ground."

" Oh, but, mother, I don't want to go, I love this place—there is my little pink bed, and my little garden, there is grandfather's home, and I have always seen him in his corner ever since I can remember."

" Grandfather will come with us, and perhaps you shall take hold of the bridle of his mule, and you will like that, won't you ? There, now, offer to help him, and tell him you will take care of his horse for him."

"Daughters, daughters," said Rodolphe, to Lucille and Martha, who went to assist him, " it is written, 'They confessed that they were pilgrims and strangers upon earth.'"

" What shall we collect of yours, father ?" said Lucille, " I have put your Bible on one side for you."

" Let nothing separate me from my best friend. I shall find those words sweeter than ever, cast into bright relief by the sombre background of sorrow—my Bible, my staff, and one or two necessaries are all that a poor old man requires."

"Here they are, grandfather," said Ardoine, "and here's another small parcel I've arranged for you, which I hope will prove useful."

"Blessings on thee, thou child of my old age; may the Lord bless thee, and guard thy young steps from all danger in these troublous times! We must look at the bright side, children. Thank God we have a place to which we can go. We shall have a warm welcome from our friends in Rora, Villar, Angrogna, and Bobi— their homes will be open to us. I trust none of us will feel biting poverty, or the want of food and the necessaries of life. 'I have been young and now am old, and yet saw I never the righteous forsaken, nor his seed begging their bread.'"

"Ah! father," replied Martha, "though

you have seen more of sorrow than we have, yet you are the most thankful, and you support us instead of our supporting you."

" Daughter, experience hath taught me the wisdom of Paul's advice, ' In everything give thanks, for this is the will of God in Christ Jesus concerning you.' "

" ' The spirit is willing,' " answered Martha, " ' but the flesh is weak,' and our hearts so cleave to the earth, that a severance is a great trial ; but He who shed the tears of nature over the grave of Lazarus will forgive us, will He not, father ?"

" Yes, dear children, He has sent this dispensation for our good, and it were no trial if we did not feel it. It would be a reproach to us not to mourn at leaving this bright home in which we have lived so many years in such singular bliss."

Rodolphe was interrupted by the entrance into the court of a man seated on a palfrey. His dress was that of a person of rank, in connection with the Papal Court, while his bland manner artfully smoothed down the caustic expression which twinkled in his calculating eye.

"Remember what I told you," whispered the Abbot of Pignerol, who, with some other monks, accompanied him; " don't be too lenient: a bold stroke just now would be true policy, and you know, Delegate, it may help the Abbot to win some of these heretics to the Apostolic Church."

The person to whom these remarks were addressed, dismounted from his horse and approached Rodolphe, whom his daughters were assisting at the other side of the court.

"Friend," said he, "I am Gastaldo. I have issued an edict in the Duke's name, but his royal Highness feels for his faithful subjects, and would, so far as his conscience will permit, relax the terms thereof."

"We thank his Highness," said Rodolphe. "It would be a boon if he would permit us to dwell on this land, which our family has owned for a hundred and fifty years."

"He knows and feels all that," replied the Delegate, "but he is obliged to appease the Church by some concession."

"It is a cruel act," retorted Raynald, sternly, "to turn us out of our houses in three days, to compel us to sell our lands at whatever sacrifice, and this in the middle of winter, when the very voice of nature intercedes for pity."

"This is true," said Gastaldo, "but have you not read the terms of the edict? Did you study it to the end? You speak as if it were peremptory. Is there no condition attached? You can avoid your sad fate; the alternative is yours."

"That of apostasy," answered Janavel.

"Never! The Duke shall command our lives, but not our consciences. Fealty to God precedes honour to the King."

"The condition is easy," continued the Delegate, "consent to go to mass, and you shall retain your house and property; your family will remain united, and your taxes and imposts shall be lightened."

"The old leaven lurks beneath," replied Rodolphe. "Abjuration or persecution, the mass or exile, are your alternatives. Then, my children, I say exile. Exile, O God, if thy providence appoints the trial; but God forbid that we should barter eternal truth for the dishonourable satisfying of the flesh."

"Yes, the mass or exile!" shouted the monks in one fierce chorus.

"Death rather than the mass," meekly replied the intrepid family circle.

"By Pope John XXIII., who agreed to sell the head of the Baptist for fifty thousand ducats!" exclaimed Malvicino, "the

Duke is right to oust such heretics, and to give their lands as a spoil to the Church. This would make a nice addition to our convent," whispered he to a grim monk near him.

" But," continued Gastaldo, " why should you be so obstinate when your interests are so plain? Look at the snow and driving rain; how will you face the winter's blast? Consider the women and children; why make them beggars and outcasts when compliance is easy? Only go to mass; after all it's shorter than your sermons; we will not ask you to chant the *Amens,* but only to show yourselves there."

" We must obey God rather than man. Liberty of conscience is our birthright, and has been guaranteed to us by charters innumerable. Even so late as May of last year, the Duke confirmed our privileges, and therefore our religion is tolerated by the law of the land."

"But our laws, thank Heaven!" said the Papal Delegate, "are not those of the Medes and Persians, which alter not; they change to suit the times, and your wisdom would be to change to suit them."

"Right and wrong alter not," replied Rodolphe; "our creed is right, and not expediency; principle before interest. We are forbidden to do evil, that good may come."

"Then you refuse the offer of the Duke's clemency?"

"If based on our apostasy, we do. We would rather imitate our fathers, and suffer for Christ's sake, than fall away from the faith delivered to us."

"Come, my daughters," said Gastaldo, addressing the women, "I doubt not you are more amenable to reason than these stubborn men. You know the charm of home; it is your heaven. What are women when vagrant and homeless?"

"Death rather than the mass!" replied

Martha and Marguerite. "We concur with our husbands, and we will beg our bread from door to door rather than sell our souls to Rome for the good things of this world."

"Children," said the crafty Inquisitor, " you do not want to leave this dear home. Should you not like to stay here, my boy?" said he, addressing Etienne.

"Yes, mother knows I should. I don't like going at all."

" You need not go, dear child, if you will say 'Jesu, Maria.' They may all stay if they will only come with us to our Church. You will come with me, won't you?"

"No, no," said the child, "I will do what mother does; I will go with grand-father; I will do what the Bible tells me to do, and I know they will try to do that."

"Well, friends," said the Delegate, "I deplore your miseries, and pity your obstinacy. You will not let the Church treat you as a tender mother, whose heart yearns to welcome back the wandering. A pleasant journey then, heretics, to you, and if you get frost-bitten, remember your heresy will one day plunge you into hell fire. The Devil take them and their obstinacy," said he to his colleagues, as he turned away. "It is surprising how Satan has kept his nest here amid these rocks and valleys so long, and how he has armed this small knot of people against the thunders of the secular power and the terrors of the Holy Office of the Apostolic Church. Surely this heresy must be what the apostle calls ' *mysterium impietatis.*' "

"Well but, Delegate, consider my plans. Ha, here are some of my faithful soldiers. By Pope John, I say, whom the Council of Constance deposed, it would be a fine thing to carry off that woman in black; I doubt not it would make the rest more willing to treat with us; and, Delegate, to be confidential, there's a girl in that house whom

I would fain win—she'll give way when her mother's caught. Say the word, for the coast is clear, and I don't see that cursed Titan in the way just now."

Without waiting for Gastaldo's assent, the Abbot whispered to his mercenaries. Five of them well armed immediately galloped into the courtyard, and seized Martha without encountering any resistance from the panic-stricken group. She was placed on a saddle before one of them, and the whole cavalcade of soldiers and ecclesiastics set themselves in motion and marched off rapidly to the capital of the valleys.

Before night Martha was a prisoner in the dungeon of the convent of La Tour.

CHAPTER XXIV.

NATURE herself seemed leagued with the Church of Rome, and armed against the children of the valleys, for the winter of 1655 was unusually severe, and violent storms added to the sufferings of the exiles.

A heavy fall of snow had taken place on the previous night; the rivers were swollen, and the plains flooded by the recent rains, with that suddenness which is always a natural phenomenon in a mountain country. The roads from St. Jean, Lucerna, Bubiano, Fenil, Briqueras, and all the other places outside the recognized boundaries, were covered as with funeral processions. Amid the blast of the mountain storms could be heard the bells of the neighbouring Roman Catholic churches, announcing the enforcement of Gastaldo's edict, and tolling, in spite of themselves, the death-knell of broken hearts and desolate homes.

Old men totter from the dwellings of their childhood, leaning on their staffs; the sick and bed-ridden are for the first time borne into the bleak mountain blast, and are laid down from time to time where the rocking pine sheds its snow-flakes on their chilled limbs; mothers with infants at their breasts wade knee-deep in snow, mud, and water; women with child, or lately confined, are taken from their beds to ford the foaming torrent, or to scale the crag; the babe must be rocked to sleep in its languishing mother's arms in the dripping cavern; little children, laden with heirlooms, faint by the way, and perish in the snow from exhaustion; the young men are not able to carry away all their property, because they bear the sick and aged; and the widow leaves her blood-stained footprints on the icy stones, still clinging to some last relic of her husband's, from which she will not be separated, even by death itself.

The band of exiles are moving from the house of La Baudène. Rodolphe's tottering steps are steadied in turn by his four daughters, who place him on his mule, and aid one another to keep him upright in his saddle. Turning round his head to take a last look at his old home, the aged patriarch sighed as he said to himself, " we have in heaven a better and an enduring substance."

Bertin, André, and Laurent carried the family Bible, one or two ornaments of old silver, and the silver cup, the token of their loyalty to their Sovereign, and of his approval.

A band of little children followed, while

the fathers who accompanied the melancholy detachment came in the rear. They
moved in silence, for their hearts were full
with heavy emotions beyond the compass
of speech, and the scalding tears which fell
to the rude ground were their mute appeal
to the God of the widow, the God to whom
vengeance belongeth.

The driving sleet almost blinded their
eyes, and the snow blocked up the road,
making their progress slow. Alas! they
were not alone. Neighbours whom they
had known for years preceded and followed
them, and the road was strewn for miles
with articles of dress and furniture.

After some time the storm swept over,
and the sunshine broke through a rent in
the clouds, as if to mock their anguish, for
sorrow tinctures all external objects with
her own hue, and Nature herself is tuneless
to a heart writhing with grief.

The Moderator, Léger, observing, not
long after, the bloody traces of his former

parishioners, fell on his knees and thanked God for their faith and constancy. The anticipation of the fruit of this cruel edict, which afforded a gleam of pleasure to the dying Marchioness, was not realized. Out of hundreds of families not one recanted to retain their property and live in peace. Out of more than two thousand exiles none apostatized, though they were deprived of earth's most precious gift—home—home—faint image of Eden's past, and bright earthly pledge of heaven to come. Their obedience and loyalty to their Sovereign were proved by their submission to this merciless edict, thereby confuting all the specious pretexts for treating them as rebels. They took joyfully the spoiling of their goods, remembering the promise to those who forsake houses and lands for Christ's sake, for many of that band could truly say, " Lord, we have left all, and followed thee."

*　　*　　*　　*　　*　　*

"Mother," said the little Aline, as she lay in Madeleine's arms, "I am cold; it rains so, why did we leave home to-day? you are quite wet."

Madeleine's heart heaved, she could make no reply. Her eye only glanced on the winding procession before her, and she felt as if the wounds of her widowhood bled afresh with greater poignancy. Covering up the child in her mantle, she walked on with pain and difficulty, as her feet were bruised against the stones, but from time to time she was obliged to sit down by the road-side, and to refresh herself with a handful of snow. Withdrawing her hood as she was seated on a stone, she looked with a mother's yearning at her helpless charge.

"Oh, my child! Sister Marguerite, look at my child, she is so cold. Speak darling," said she, clasping Aline to her bosom, that some of her own vital warmth might be imparted to the little one.

Aline opened her eyes slowly, and as they met those of her mother a faint smile overspread her pale features, a smile sadder than that which touched the mother's heart as her darling lay before her in the cradle. The mother rocked herself to and fro as she clasped the child.

"Here is something," she exclaimed after a pause. "Dear Ardoine has given me a little bottle of wine; that will revive her. Look, darling, this is what cossy Ardy has sent for you." So saying, Madeleine raised the child's head with her left arm, and poured a few drops of the cordial into her mouth. A flush as of returning life overspread her face, and she appeared refreshed.

The mother covered her from the scattered snow and rain which still fell, and moved on slowly, leaning upon Marguerite's arm.

"Oh, Marguerite," said she after a little time, "my child feels heavier. Oh,

I touched it—it is so cold! Look, its eyes are closed; it is—it is dead!" So saying, Madeleine fainted, and fell prostrate in the snow upon the body of Aline, which she still encircled in her arms.

Raynald and Janavel soon came up to render what assistance they could, and Marguerite was unweary in chafing her sister's temples. The little corpse was carried with them, for they were loth to commit her to a grave by the roadside. The child lay stiff and cold, her dark hair encrusted with snow, her lips colourless and half-opened, her eyes closed.

It is painful to a mother to weep over a babe when taken from her amid every alleviation, but much more painful was it to suffer such a loss as a bitter first fruit of exile, and as a pledge of a more agonizing future.

*   *   *   *   *   *

"O Lord! remember thy servants; enter their tears in thy book of remem-

brance. Show to whom vengeance belongeth! When thou makest inquisition for
blood, forget not thy martyrs; remember
the silent griefs of broken hearts and deso-
lated homes, as well as the groans of those
who have perished at the stake, in the
dungeon, or on the remorseless rack."

"O Lord, to whom vengeance belongeth; O God, to whom vengeance
belongeth, shew thyself!

"Lift up thyself, thou Judge of the
earth; render a reward to the proud.

"Let the heavens rejoice, and let the
earth be glad; let the sea roar, and the
fulness thereof.

"Let the field be joyful, and all that is
therein; then shall all the trees of the
wood rejoice

"Before the Lord; for He cometh, FOR
HE COMETH TO JUDGE THE EARTH: He shall
judge the world with righteousness, and
the people with his truth."

CHAPTER XXV.

THE MISSIONARIES OF THE VATICAN.

THE archiepiscopal town of Pignerol, en-
trenched among the offshoots of the Alps,
and situated on the frontier of the valleys,
is not without its memories in the blood-
stained persecutions of the Waldenses. Its
dungeons have echoed with the screams of
the victim and with the prayers of the
saint, and its principal square has often
been illumined by the lurid flame, the
fiery chariot of some martyred soul to the
presence of its God.

Its institutions were peculiar, and
worthy the genius of that religion which
tramples upon human nature, as well as on

things divine, when antagonistic to her despotic tyranny. A hospital existed for the reception of Waldensian children, who, having been decoyed from their parents, were compulsorily reared in the Romish faith. This expedient was the device of Father Bonaventure and the Prior Rorengo, who boasts of it in his historical memoirs. In the Patents of Grace of 1655, the only protection which the Waldenses could obtain was, that boys should not be violently taken from their parents under twelve, nor girls under ten years of age.

Pignerol had also its Monte de Pieta, an establishment for lending money on pledges, which were cancelled only in times of deep distress, on condition of the heretic abjuring, and giving his soul in pawn to Popery.

The abbey of the Franciscan monks had long been distinguished for their inveterate rancour against their heretical neighbours, and they retained in their pay a body of armed bandits, who were in the habit of making incursions into the valleys to kidnap the children, to plunder the houses, to devastate the country, or to massacre individuals.

About midday on the twenty-eighth of January, a party of monks, accompanied by some Piedmontese and Irish soldiers, started from the abbey of Pignerol. An expression of fierce joy was visible on the countenances of the monks, as they contemplated a lucrative campaign among the heretics on this day of ejection. Their uproarious mirth was, however, suddenly arrested as they passed one of those repulsive crosses which still disfigure the roadsides of enthralled Italy. Opposite to the cross was a small shrine, where a lamp was burning before the picture of the Virgin. Uncovering, the band of felons crossed themselves, and, falling on their knees, remained for some moments ·in silent adoration, while the monk at their head mumbled some scraps of Latin.

" By St. Pathrick's thumbscrews," said one to his companion, as they approached the entrance of the valley of Lucerna, " what's this Goshen we're promised here to make up for Ould Ireland. Shure, then, we must be ready to labour in the extermination of heretics."

" The land looks well, Misther Donoghue ; those high mountains are bigger than our Magillicuddys Reeks ; but I fear we shall not get as good a dhrap of ould *potheen* here."

" Well, Michael O'Flanaghan, I would swear by Moran's chain, I, a well-knit Irishman, who trace my gintle blood right up through my mother's breed to our first parent, if I get a good berth here, I'll brew as good a dhrap as ever you dhrank with Misther O'Callaghan in your cabin on the turf bog."

" By Saint Patrick's toothpick," said

the second speaker, "here's a roomy shebeen shop. Halloa, Fathers, *Patres conscripti*, as my young masther used to say," cried he, addressing the monks; "faith, I want to see if there's a jewel of a girl here can darn my rags, for the snow sthrikes could right through."

"Och! Michael, you ould sinner, and that's the game you're up to when your ould hen's not looking. You niver dare give the top o' the morning to ony if her weasel eyes were on ye."

"Well, well, O'Donoghue, say nothing about it, but tell me jist how you got here into this counthry?"

"Agragh! you know what took place in 41 in Ould Ireland; jist fourteen birthdays ago I'm reckoning. We Catholics did our duty; we settled some forty or fifty thousand of the Protestant dogs. Arrah! thin, lave me alone for scrimmagin,—shure my finger inds were rid with English blood, and as his riverince

told us, we washed our footsteps in the
blood of the ungodly. Glory be to God!
Well, we knocked up and down for
some time, like two weathercocks on
two Catholic and Protestant churches
on opposite sides of the sthreet, which can't
agree together to tell you how the wind
runs. We knocked about, says I, till this
Puritan—ould Noll they call him—stepped
over to the isle six years ago—in '49 that
would be, for I'm a bit of a scholar—and
by the jawbone of Patrick, the serpent-
killer, he thrashed us, and he then told
us we could turn out; and I heard that
forty thousand of our boys have left the
ould counthry. There's a lot of us here,
and they say if we can root up these heretics, ould Savoy will give us their places."

"Father!" shouted the Irishman again
in a loud voice, "*avante sinistra*, to the
right I mean, let's visit this house. Dust
my teeth, doesn't he ondersthand his own
jargon."

The monks, in compliance with the man's hint, turned off the road, and took the path leading into the farm of La Baudène. The Abbot Malvicino was dismounting in the courtyard, having returned in hopes of finding Ardoine.

"Soldiers of the Cross!" said he, addressing his ragged followers as they entered, "the Holy Church bids you welcome here; spoil the Egyptians, and see if there's anything here you would like to take home as a keepsake from the Pope of Rome."

"Shure and be gawnies I can find a somethin—so here goes—God and the blissed Mither, and the thrue Church for iver."

The soldiers dispersed over the farm, and began the work of pillage. Most of the family were away, having left early in the day; but Jean and a few children had remained to minister to the wants of Marie, for whose removal arrangements were being made. The soldiers speedily bound Jean hand and foot, while the frightened children precipitately hid themselves as best they could in the outbuildings. After eating and drinking what they could find, the rabble began with zest the work of demolition. The furniture of the house was broken and thrown into the courtyard, the windows were smashed, the woodwork torn from the walls, relics of affection, mute things which had consoled the mourner's heart, were cast into the mire, and trampled under foot.

The revelry and oaths of the soldiers reached Marie, who trembled at the thought of the indignities to which she might be subjected by a brutal soldiery.

"Comrade!" said O'Donoghue, "we've niver been up-stairs. Here is another house, with rags over the windows; perhaps the *barbets* have some gowld here. I can do a powerful sthroke o' business for my ain belongins."

"Not much of that," said a Piedmontese soldier, Cattalin by name; "not much gold or silver waiting for owners in this den, I trow."

The idea of plunder acted on the confused brain of three or four half-drunken bystanders, who rushed into Marie's room to search for the supposed spoil. On entering the chamber they were involuntarily startled as they beheld that figure, so white and motionless. O'Donoghue's superstitions overcame him, and hastily crossing himself, he fell on his knees, muttering—

"Ave Maria! Rosary of the Vargin! Holy Bridget! have marcy on me and purtect us!"

"By the rags of Peter the Hermit, those dogs have left behind them a corpse for us to bury," said Villalmin Roche, advancing to the bed.

"Oh, Pathrick!" said O'Donoghue, "oh, Pathrick! who griped the last viper on the banks of the Boyne, take care of my sinful body."

"Nay, nay, you need order no second-hand coffins," cried Cattalin, "he's not dead, man ; look how he winces under the point of my sword."

"It's a woman, by the middle knuckle of St. Francis!" cried O'Donoghue, his courage returning. "It's not you, young gallant, will hurt the lady. Convert her now, and lead her into heaven to the Blessed Virgin."

"I say, old lamb of Beersheba," said Cattalin, bending over her, "the Pope of Rome hath sent us to save your soul. Be quick, and say your prayers; say 'Jesu Maria;' and lift up your hand here, old aunt," continued he, moving the suf- ferer's arm, "and cross yourself this fashion—here right, left—left, right."

"Come, be quick," said Villalmin Roche, "or we'll throw you into the court- yard for an airing, and then pour you out

some hot toast and water. If not, old
Father Malvicino will speak to his private
confessor with horns, and he'll give you
some hot toast without water."

This sally was received with a burst of
brutal laughter, and the floor of the room
trembled under the stamping of the soldiers' feet.

"I say," pursued Cattalin, "change
caps with me; do lend me that nightcap
for our drummer-boy. I should just like
to see her in my helmet, that I may see
how I look myself."

"*Cospetto!* leave the old dame alone,"
said Villalmin, "I want to do the spiritual
thing. You've not long for this world,
mother, St. Francis is beckoning you into
Paradise. Will you go?"

"Yes," cried out the man. "St.
Francis, we'll save a soul in your name
—wait a moment, she'll come before
long. Call out 'Jesu Maria,' and then
cross yourself, for Peter can't be kept

standing outside in the cold waiting for
you."

"Lord Jesus!" gasped the sufferer,
"receive my spirit. Is the chariot of fire
waiting for my soul? but a breath, and I
shall be with Thee face to face in heaven.
Lord Jesus! come quickly."

"Halt! no harangues, old woman;
pray to the Virgin. Now, boys, we must
have a toast:—' *Viva la Santa Chiesa Romana!*'"

The chorus of voices brake forth into
one unearthly roar at the given signal.

"*E viva la sante fede!*" continued the
speaker, and again the Pope's disciples
strained their lungs in sending their voices
to heaven.

"*E guai agli Barbetti,*" once more
pealed harshly on the sufferer's ear.

"Now, mother," continued Villalmin,
"if you won't pray we'll make you."

"You can do what you will with my
body, it's a poor crumbling tabernacle,

long fitted for the tomb; but my soul is safe in the hands of my Saviour, whose blood has washed me from all sin, and on whose death and merits I can calmly rely now and in the hour of death."

"Come, come, old fellow," said Lemna, "it's a shame for a man to vex a woman, and you're too ugly to convert her; the look of such as you would make her take an oath not to be on the same side with you; the sight of you would save me ten scudi a year in making vinegar."

"Mind your own business, you Bologna butcher, don't you see I mean the woman good? I want to get her soul into heaven, and you, you haven't grace enough to wish her there, as you know you'll never have a pass to get there yourself."

"Come, mother, say 'Jesu Maria,' and cross," cried O'Donoghue; "I'm hoarse with hallooing—quick, or I'll give you a dig with my sword to brighten your wits. I'm listening," and the man bent his head to catch her words, presenting a strange contrast with his huge shock of red hair and ragged garments to the death-like form that lay on the bed.

His patience was on the wane; his eyes sparkled with religious frenzy, and he was about to proceed to some act of violence. He seized the sufferer; but the icy touch, and the exceeding lightness of the body appalled him, and he released her from his grasp.

"How, now, sons," said the Abbot Malvicino, entering the room, "what's this plunder you've got?—is it a living soul?—then that's for me. Away ye lads, look after your stomachs. Leave her to me, and by Pope Benedict IX., who sold St. Peter's chair, I'll soon make a disciple of her, and add another member to the Holy Catholic and Apostolic Church."

That rough Franciscan when left alone felt for a moment the associations of suffering—in the presence of that female whose look was so unearthly, and whose unnatural paleness was deepened by her fears.

"Holy Pope Gregory," said Malvicino, crossing himself, "she looks like a corpse stolen from some *campo santo*, a sister it may be of the cadaverous Rorengo. But methinks it will not be difficult to make a convert of this weak vessel, and women's souls make up one's score as well as men's, and it will blot out some of my sins. Mother," said he, advancing towards her, "I hope I recognize in you a sister in the faith, one who is in the fold of the Church, out of which there is no salvation."

"I trust," replied the sufferer, "that I am in the Church of which Christ is the chief corner stone."

"But I mean, do you belong to his visible Church, the Holy Roman, which God established by St. Peter, and governs by his Vicar the Pope."

"No; I do not belong to the Romish

Church, but to that apostolic branch which has always existed in these valleys."

"Will you imperil your soul? Unless you are a believer in the mass, your salvation is impossible."

"I rely upon the Word of God; I read nothing there about the mass, so I can do without it. Jesus Christ is my rock, and on his death and merits I securely rest. I have lain here for twenty-one years, and I can trust my Saviour to the last."

"Oh," said the monk aside, "we have a controversialist here. These *barbets* seem to instruct their people with their lying sophistries, so that they are able to perplex even the advocates of truth."

"Woman," said he, raising his voice, "I have come to save you. If you will not let me do it by persuasion, I shall excommunicate you, and hand you over to the soldiers of the cross."

"'O Lord, have mercy on my soul! O Christ, forsake me not! To Thee will

I look, thou God of my salvation!   In the hour of death hold my right hand, saying unto me, Fear not, I am with thee.'"

"Woman, will you repent?   Will you abjure your heresy?   Say '*Ave Maria,*' and then I will befriend you and your relations."

"You speak to one who is at the point of death, and almost sees the better city; worldly motives are worthless when we approach the grave."

"What," said the monk, "are you obstinate?   Here, Father Placido Corso, lend us your spiritual aid, help me to drag this daughter into the kingdom."

"Gently, Abbot," said the priest; "the poor thing is weak and ill, treat her gently.   It is no credit to our faith to use violence with such feeble vessels."

"There's no other way with them but decision.   If you can't bend, you must break; at least that is the teaching of the Holy Office."

"To convince her argue with her, and tell her what the Holy Fathers have said."

"She doesn't care for the Fathers, nor the Councils. These heretics put their faith only in what the Bible teaches."

"Then argue with her out of the Bible, you know enough of it, don't you, to vindicate our doctrines?"

"I don't think I do; I only know some of those parts I chant by heart, and if it comes to bandying texts of Scripture, by Pope Celestin III., who kicked the Emperor Henry VI.'s crown off his head, I shall come off the worst. But go and look after your belongings, and leave me with my erring daughter."

Malvicino went up to Marie, and holding the crucifix against her lips, said—

"So you refuse to belong to the Holy Roman Church, and talk about your cursed heresy, which has clung to these infernal valleys so long. Then the devil take your soul and body."

Bending over the bed he spit in that wan face, and raised his hand as if to inflict a blow. A fierce glare passed over his features, which suddenly relaxed into a smile, as if some happy thought had suggested itself.

"Good," said he, aloud, "that will be a work of supererogation, and the blessed Bridget will intercede for me after this. I will—I will save her—I will baptize her into the true Church."

With these words he began to search about the room, and at last found some water, which he poured into a cup. Kneeling by the bedside, and making the sign of the cross, he chanted in a monotonous tone, "*Baptizo te in nomine Domini, et Filii, et Spiritûs Sancti*. Amen." Then making the sign of the cross on her forehead, he emptied the contents of the cup upon Marie's head.

"I have saved her—I have saved her," muttered he to himself as he quitted the apartment.

CHAPTER XXVI.

DURING the monk's interview with Marie the lawless rabble held undisputed possession of the building, without any check upon their wanton brutality.

Among the soldiers Michael O'Flanagan was conspicuous for his violence, his Celtic passions having been thoroughly aroused by the work of destruction and plunder.

"Och, was there iver sich a place?" he shouted: "'tis a sore day with me since I brathed this air, but I'll smash somebody's head, as we do at Donnybrook. There's no shillelahs here. Wisha, an' ye may travel many a long mile afore ye gets the likes o' me. Be geminy! give me that picthure of that milky-haired man—I'll put his eye out."

With these words he dashed an earthenware jug against the wall, which was shivered to pieces. He then leaped upon the table, and with his sword drawn harangued the bystanders.

"Brother," said Placido Corso to Malvicino, "this mad Irishman may strike our noses with the end of that sword he's whirling about. You seem as if you were looking for some one."

"By Pope Leo X. and his holy indulgences, I'm looking for a girl I saw here the other day. Ah! now I think of it," continued the Abbot to himself, "I must be careful. Echard has the enforcement of the edict, and he might come in here and spoil my plans. I must keep him out of the way. In this case I had better return to La Tour or Pignerol. I have told my people to keep their eyes about them and capture her."

"Ah!" said O'Flanagan, addressing Malvicino, "Och, holy Abbot, you look frightened. Be aisy; though my bones ache from the beggarly mat you gave me to lie on last night. Well, well, forgive and forget. Here's hurrah for the Pope of Rome—does he say his prayers in bed? I know he'd like to sip a glass of Irish whisky. Shure how could he keep his throat up to the work of blessin' if he did not wet it? He's right, the Vicar; here, boys, you're for the Pope. Is there none of the rale stuff here, to give his Holiness a dhrap? Hurrah for ould Ireland. I say, mavourneen, what's in there? I want to look in this cellar — is there any bin of St. Patrick's brew here? if so you shall let me go halves."

O'Flanagan then rushed into the courtyard, tumbling over the ruins that lay in every direction. He vowed vengeance

against all Turks and Infidels, and swore
that he would run through the heretic who
would not cross himself.

"Cross yourself, man," said he, addressing Jean, who was a prisoner, "are
you cowld? Ah! well, ye see these monks
are lighting you a blaze with yer own sticks.
Faiths, get out of the way, and you'll see
we Irish of the ould blood are as thrue to
the Mither of God on this side the Channel
as on the other."

Reeling about O'Flanagan reached the
staircase which led to Marie's room.

"We'll go up," said he, "into this den.
If I don't find any dhrink here, I'll git up
a blaze on my own account."

With his rough fist he shattered the
panel of Marie's door. The ruffian stood
upon the threshold of the sick room, where
all, before this day, had entered with bated
breath and heartfelt sympathy, and he pealed
forth a stanza of his Bacchanalian song, in
a spot where nought but hallowed prayer

and praise had been heard for years. Pushing the door aside he entered the room, and his eye rested upon that apparent image of death. He was riveted when he saw that blanched and death-like face, shaded by her dark hair, and whose dimmed eyes plaintively appealed to the sympathy of those who enjoyed the blessing of unclouded sight.

The Irish fanatic stood speechless; for a moment there was a death-like silence in that sick room, broken at intervals by the shouts and tumult of the soldiers in the court.

A change of expression softened O'Flanagan's features, and reproduced for a moment that look of innocence which was once the ornament of his boyish days. The wild, maddened glare of that eye had relapsed into one of melancholy thoughtfulness, as if memories bound deep within his heart were touched, and his soul was brooding over an awakened past. For some time he stood in silence, without moving, and gazed on Marie until tears stole down his weather-beaten cheeks.

It was a triumph due to the calm majesty of suffering, a proof of that axiom that under the bandit's rough exterior there yet beats a human heart—that heart through which we taste more than a solitary existence.

"Thank Heaven!" said he, "that I have not spoiled her, and that I've not let those other ruffians hurt her. Shure I would not touch one hair of her head. Ah! she's like her mavourneen. Is it herself that I see, or am I still draming? No, I see the white body, the hair, the thin hand—it's my mither! Oh, mither! I thought I had left ye in that cabin that looks o'er the pool in county Fermanagh. Look! it must be herself; the pale cheek, the closed eye, the silence brings her before me. Ah!" said the young man, burying his head in his hands and bursting into tears, " how happy I was thin ! My dear mither, you're a long way off from me now; och ! I know not if you're alive, and before I went soldierin', and saw the rough side of life, I was your favourite boy. Shure at my very worst time I trembled before your tears, and when I was lavin' you made me kneel down by your bedside, looking jist the same as yon sick crathur ; and thin, as you were blind, you axed where your boy was, and you put your thin hand on his head, and felt my face,—you did, you did. Oh, if you are dead, you will have remimbered me with your dying breath. Mither, I did not think to see you again so far off."

" Lord Jesus !" said a plaintive voice, " sit by my furnace. Thou art my anchor, which entereth within the vail. Leave me not, or if the hour has come, speak the word, for my soul waiteth."

" Harm you ! is that what you're saying in your foreign tongue ? I won't, though the Pope himself were urging me on. I'll purtect you for the sake of my dear ould mither, whose last words were, ' Avick, trat iverybody as you'd have them trat you.' "

The guileless memories of an early home, which often draw a tear even from the criminal on his last night in the condemned cell, appeared to have changed the nature of O'Flanagan, for his heart, that centre of mystery, had been touched. He moved gently about the room, and proceeded to arrange the dismantled chamber, turning his head from time to time to glance at the bed. With the delicacy of a woman's touch he moistened her lips, and in tones of kindness soothed her fears, though his Celtic exhortations, with its sparse Italian sprinkling, were lost upon the sufferer.

" Wisha, thin, 'tis meself that will help you for my mither's sake," he soliloquized; " shure your own folks will come back to fetch you out of harm's way; asthore !

they'll never lave you alone long. Ah! what a scrimmage those other plunderin' rascals have made here!"

Standing at the door, he drove back the rioters, who attempted to mount the stairs, and kept guard until the bugle sounded, when the soldiers and the monks proceeded to the convent of La Tour, taking with them Jean as their prisoner, and the children who had not escaped at their first approach.

"Farewell, mavourneen, and may the Holy Vargin kape you and have mercy on ye for my ould sick mither's sake!"

So saying, he joined his companions, whose oaths and ribaldry fell more harshly on his ear than before, from the purer association which had been revived within his breast.

"Flanagan," said Malvicino, addressing the Irishman, "I've a small commission for you. Gallop to Pignerol, and you will meet an officer of the Duke's, Echard by name, who has authority to enforce the edict; he will be accompanied by some soldiers. I don't want him to come to this farm, for reasons connected with the interests of the Holy Church. Either send him at once to La Tour, because Gastaldo wants him, or else back to Pignerol to the abbey to meet me. Do you understand? ride with him, but keep him from going into the farm on any account."

With these instructions, O'Flanagan left his companions, and rode back alone in the direction of Pignerol.

CHAPTER XXVII.

DAGOT.

THE tramp of the horses, and the roar of human voices gradually died away, and silence reigned throughout the farm of La Baudène, broken only by the murmuring of the Pelice in the distance. It was an ominous silence, akin to that of the grave, a strange contrast to the previous riot, and to the former buoyant joy of that social hearth, upon which Gastaldo's signature had begun to wreak its baneful desolation.

Malvicino, who was obliged to return to Gastaldo at La Tour, had summoned his soldiers to accompany him, hoping to be able to return to La Baudène later in the day. In his reverie how to carry out his purpose in case O'Flanagan should disappoint him, he met Dagot and some other soldiers going in the direction of the farm.

"Friend Dagot," whispered the Abbot, addressing the soldier apart, "I've a little affair which I will entrust you with, whereby you can win your Holy Father's blessing. Go to La Baudène, and if you can find a good-looking girl, with golden ——. Ha, you were once quartered there, and therefore you know her well. Secure the girl for a friend of mine, and I'll shorten your time in purgatory. Above all, take care of that young officer Echard, and keep her out of his way, should he chance to come to the farm in the fulfilment of his duties—do you understand? then there's a ducat to toast the Pope."

"Thanks, holy Abbot," said the man with a grin, "I'll cater for the flesh, and you for the spirit. What a fool he must think me !" continued he to himself, as he rode away, " if he thinks I don't see through him, and am going to do his work. No, Dagot must look after his own interests if fortune gives him the chance. Ah! I see the old place again; I'll run that fellow Raynald through if I can."

"Comrade," said Dagot, addressing Berru, " I see the farm before us where we were quartered. Now's the time to see if we can pick up any spoil there, for I believe the edict of Gastaldo turns them out."

"Ha, ha!" replied Berru, "you still keep up old memories. I'm afraid that girl is entering into your calculations, but take my advice and don't burn your fingers."

"Halloa!" said Dagot, as he saw Ardoine entering the court-yard, " there's my old flame; I hope I shall have better luck this time, if I pop the question. Pity we've left our priest behind, or he could have earned his fees before vespers."

Ardoine, who had left her mother for a short time, to assist in finding a litter for her removal, had returned with the promptitude of affection as soon as possible, and had preceded the soldiers whom she had not noticed in the distance. Her heart trembled as she entered the court-yard, and saw the signs of havoc and destruction on all sides. It was evident that a party of soldiers had been there in the absence of the family, though from the melancholy silence which reigned throughout the place, they and everybody else seemed to have departed.

With impatient eagerness she flew to her mother's room, and was relieved to find her in her accustomed place. Wiping her forehead she gently pressed her hands, and kissed her parched lips.

"Mother, mother, my heart upbraids me for having left you at all; but uncle thought I could best arrange about the litter. I hope you are safe and well, and have not found my absence long. I have come back as soon as I could."

"I am so glad to see you, beloved child. God deals gently with me; my heart over-flows with love to Him, and is kept in perfect peace. I cleave ·to Jesus without a murmur or a doubt. You don't know with what delight I look for his coming, for the sting of death has been taken away by his precious cross."

"You look pale and frightened, dear mother. I fear from what I see that some of the roving bands of soldiers have been here, many of whom are to and fro on the road. Thank God, they have done you no harm. How unfortunate that our brave men are away!"

"Some soldiers have been here, daughter," said Marie, not wishing to ex-cite Ardoine's fears, "but the conduct of one of them was indeed strange. God must have touched his heart: he burst violently into the room, and I thought I should have been killed, when his whole manner was suddenly changed, and he moistened my lips, and did all he could to protect and cheer me."

"How strange!" said Ardoine, musingly.

"Blessed be God!" continued Marie; "He does not leave us in our trials, but is able at all times to give us out of his fulness what we need. Oh, how sweet to have a Saviour's bosom to recline on! I long to be with Him, for the sting of death is gone, and even now I live beneath his smiles. Daughter, you don't know with what delight I look for his approach; but thanks be to Him I have still patience given me to wait his time."

"Mother," said Ardoine, after a pause, "I wonder that I don't see Uncle Jean and any of the children about. Where can they have gone? I feel quite frightened. Oh, Janavel and Raynald, where are you? forsake us not."

"My daughter, calm yourself. Take

my Bible, child, and read to me from its blessed pages."

" I will, mother ; shall I read at any particular place ?"

" Read something my Saviour said, for comfort flows to me from every page of God's Word, but especially from Christ's words ; they make my soul burn. I love a chapter though it be full of names, for I know it is from God. Oh, nothing in the world is so dear to me as God's Word ! it is dearer than thousands of gold and silver ; it imparts such a blessedness to the soul. I have tasted it, and know it is so sweet from experience. I wish to feel Christ in the Bible speaking afresh to me, and then when I contemplate Christ in his Word, and what He has done for me, my soul wants to burst its bonds, and soar on wings above, beyond this present world."

Marie was suddenly interrupted by the door being burst violently open, and the

dreaded mercenary Dagot rushed into the
room. He flew towards Ardoine, who was
on her knees by her mother's bedside, with
her hands clasped, and her head resting
upon the open Bible. At the sound of
those footsteps terror paled her cheek,
making its hue almost as blanched as that
of the wan sufferer. As she fell at Dagot's
feet and besought pity for herself and her
mother, she might have given Raphael a
model of an unfallen angel supplicating for
a fallen world.

"Ah, I have found you at last, and a
long search I have had for you. I thought
you'd not be far off that old hag, who I
heard lay sweltering here. You left me
in the river last time, did you, when your
lover was by? But now it is my turn, and
by the Virgin I'll have my revenge. Well,
don't be afraid, my little bird, I'll treat you
gently. I've been a bachelor this five-and-
forty years, because I could not mate, but
this is the girl for the Frenchman Dagot.

What, won't you come quietly? Then I must help you."

So saying, he seized her in his arms, and dragged her downstairs to another side of the building.

"My pretty maid, fear not. I will find our priest to tie the holy knot between us. But we can postpone that for fear of accidents, and then the conscience of a heretic need not regret a Frenchman and a Catholic."

Ardoine screamed and struggled, but it was of no avail. She was in the grasp of one whom plunder and passion had aroused to madness, and the blackness of despair seemed to have sealed her fate.

CHAPTER XXVIII.

THE RESCUE.

ECHARD had been appointed by the Marquis of Pianesse to conduct some troops from Turin to La Tour and its neighbourhood, to be used if necessary for the enforcement of Gastaldo's edict.

It was not until the afternoon of the 28th that he approached the scene of his mission. He had fallen somewhat behind his detachment, when he was met by the Irish soldier, Michael O'Flanagan, whom Malvicino · had sent to intercept or divert his route.

"Och, in troth there's jist the man I'm saking. I'll be afther telling him all about it. Plase yer honor there's been a great row in the farm hard by on yonder road, and if you could do them a sarvice I should be obleeged to you. In one of the rooms there's one like the ghost of my mither, poor sowl. She's one of them six sisthers, and ould father, the Abbot, sint me to tell you not to come there ; and I'll discharge my mission, descinded as I am from the kings of Connaught, by my mither's side. But yer'd do a power o' good if you did go, and might save some poor girl. If those be your soldiers, some of them have gone in there, for I saw some cattle standin' about. O misther, go and see if ye can do any good, but remimber I towld you what the Abbot towld me, to tell ye not to go there. I did, I did, as I'm the last mimber of the race of the kings of Connaught."

Echard did not wait to hear more, for his humanity prompted him to do all in his power to mitigate the severities and horrors which would inevitably attend this wholesale and sudden eviction. Seeing some of his men near the farm of La Baudène, he concluded that it was the house to which O'Flanagan referred, and on entering recognized it as the place where he had been three days before. The little he had then seen of the family had interested him, and he remembered the romantic account of their patriarchal union and singular habits of life. The scene of devastation in the court that met his eye needed no interpreter, while the curses and oaths of the soldiers attested too faithfully the riot of the messengers of death. He hastened to find the sufferer to whom O'Flanagan referred. From the Irishman's directions he soon found the outbuilding, and mounting the stairs advanced to Marie's bedside, threading his way amid the broken furniture.

"Good lady," he whispered in a gentle voice, "do not be afraid, I am an officer of the Duke; I will take care that none of these soldiers hurt you. I will stand at your door and protect you myself."

"My daughter," articulated the sufferer with difficulty, "my Ardoine, save her! Oh, sir, a mother's heart beseeches you! They have taken her away. My daughter, my daughter! Hasten and save her."

After the first burst of grief, Marie appeared to recover herself, and clasping her hands whispered, "Father, forgive me. I will drink the cup that my Father puts into my hands to the dregs; it is mingled with love. The more I suffer, the more I rejoice in Christ my Saviour. All flows from infinite love, which I feel through the power of the Holy Ghost. 'God is love'!"

"Christ's righteousness is seamless," continued the sufferer, after a pause, with unusual emphasis; "I have no fears of death, for Christ is all-sufficient. He is my anchor. He has paid all my debts, and therefore I have peace. I have no hope in myself. His merits are my plea, and with this I can calmly enter into eternity. 'Thanks be unto God for his unspeakable gift! God is love'!"

The officer stood silent, as if debating how he could assist her, and evidently struck with the warm heart-breathings which issued from that corpse-like form, while his lips mechanically repeated her last words, "'God is love'!"

He had hardly left the room before several of his soldiers, with fearful oaths and uproar, began to mount the stairs.

"Back," cried Echard, in a tone of command; "soldiers, you know your officer, back; sound the bugle; to horse; for we must on to La Tour."

Abashed at this unexpected order, the men descended the wooden staircase with heavy tramp, muttering oaths against him who had marred their plans.

Echard turned, and gently lifted the latch, in order to reassure the sufferer. He

went to the couch, and in a whisper exhorted her not to tremble, for he would protect her at the risk of his life. Receiving
no answer, he bent over the body, when,
to his surprise, he found that she was a
corpse. Marie had silently fallen asleep in
Jesus, in the midst of the tumult and blas-
phemy that had desecrated that once peaceful home. The longed-for moment, which
summed up her twenty-one years' captivity,
had come at last. It had come suddenly
and swiftly. For years the vigils of love
had been incessantly kept by her bedside,
but when death came she was alone. None
heard her sigh of severance; none bowed
to catch her farewell speech. None learned
her last experiences, nor sighed to mark
the glazing film of death overspreading her
eyes. A smile lingered on her features, as
if at the last some bright foretaste of heaven
had flooded her heart when ceasing to beat,
a smile more plaintive because begotten in
death, and leaving its impress upon that

forlorn and tenantless body to typify
victory over the grave. Echard paused as
he gazed on that spectral face, and im-
printed its last expression upon his memory.
He had beheld death on the field of battle
in all its varied shapes of horror, but he
felt a thrill as of a mystic spell, a calm
wafting of his own soul to heaven, as he
came in contact with the King of Terrors,
so noiseless, so tranquil, and apparently so
welcome in that lone chamber.

The scene of the last death-bed he had
witnessed a few weeks before recurred
forcibly to his mind. He had there seen
one endowed with rank and fortune, and
noted for her religious zeal, struggling with
death. Yet, what were her experiences?
Fearfulness, and a horrible dread over-
whelmed her; imprecations and cries of
agony came from those lips on which the
last word was "blood!" Her heart was filled
with dissatisfaction and fear; the proud
Marchioness trembled before her Judge,

and all the usual appalling adjuncts of death had been heightened in the case of her he called mother. But in this obscure chamber peace seemed to hallow death; a joy and bright desire had flooded that spirit whose last utterance was "'God is love'!" His breast heaved, as he contrasted the two scenes, and heard the voice of conscience suggesting which was the most worthy of God and of pure religion.

"Strange utterance!" said Echard to himself; "'God is love'! when things look so much the reverse. The religion which can produce such fruits cannot be so thoroughly bad as our Church represents."

Laying his hand on that cold forehead, and closing his eyes, he involuntarily breathed a prayer as he murmured her last words, "'God is love'!"

In the midst of his reflections, he was startled at hearing piercing cries in the court-yard: they were the voices of pursuer and pursued. He listens: he hastens to the stairs. The cries approach; the pursued flies across the court-yard, the pursuer follows. Ardoine's feet scarce touch the ground; Dagot's hand all but grasps her garments. In unreasoning despair she makes for her mother's room; she sees some one before her. He has on the uniform of Savoy; honour may lurk in his breast: she must trust him. "Oh save me! save me! Oh mother, mother, save me, save me!"

A glance at the girl was enough to interest Echard in her fate. It must be the daughter. To draw his sword and intercept the soldier was the act of a moment.

"Back, villain!" shouted Echard, addressing Dagot, who was mounting the stairs; "stand back, and leave the girl alone. Back, or I'll hurl you back!"

"Will you?" said Dagot, whom drink and fury had half maddened. "Will you? then take that!" So saying, he seized his arquebus, and fired at Echard.

The gathering twilight, and Dagot's unsteady aim, saved the officer. The shot grazed his thigh, causing him to reel backwards. Dagot pressed on, but Echard, whose sword was drawn, made a lunge forward, and drove it through the wretched man's breast. There was an awful groan; a stream of blood deluged the stairs, and the red drops trickled from the sword as it was withdrawn from the body.

"Mother of God!" said the man. "I'm killed. Holy Virgin, save me!" and the soldier fell heavily backwards, and lay motionless at the foot of the stairs.

Casting one contemptuous glance upon the fallen man, Echard entered the chamber of death to reassure the object of his pity.

" The red drops trickled from the sword as it was withdrawn from the body."

Page 344.

CHAPTER XXIX.

ARDOINE had fallen senseless near the door; Echard bent over her with the kindly feelings of a protector, and his gaze rested for the first time upon her countenance. The eyes were shut, the cheek was pale, the golden hair was dishevelled, but a mystic charm environed her and fascinated Echard's heart. He needed not the inspirations of death, yea, of the mother's corpse to prompt him to be the daughter's champion, for the sanctity of innocence and the silent advocacy of beauty stirred his generous nature. He placed her gently on the sofa, turning her so that she should not receive a shock from beholding that lifeless form. It was some time before consciousness returned. Did he find those moments tedious? He would have hastened her recovery had he been able, but did he regret having the opportunity of gazing upon that face without causing it to quail, and of imprinting its features upon his heart? He felt what he had never felt before—a strange interest riveted him; an unbidden passion seized his soul, and he was no longer the same as when he first entered that room.

After some time Ardoine gradually recovered and opened her eyes.

"Where am I? Alas! I remember. Is it a dream? Mother, dearest, I am with you; are you safe? Oh, sir, forgive my wanderings; fear has almost deprived me of my senses. Was it you upon whom I cast myself to escape the soldier's grasp? How have I been saved? You look as if your heart was not iron, and as if a woman's tears might touch you."

Grasping his hand she pressed it to her lips. She dropped it, however, when her modesty realized her position, and caused her to restrain her expression of gratitude; but their eyes had met, their hands had touched, and an electric thrill caused Echard to tremble throughout his whole frame.

"Calm yourself, sister, calm yourself; you are safe under my care—it was I who rescued you on the stairs; I have punished the villain in a way he will not forget, if he lives," added he in a lower tone, "to remember it."

"I hope you have not killed him. What is that by your side? It's your sword, and it is red. O heavens, what scenes are taking place in our beloved home! Grandfather and aunts, where are you all?"

"Do not excite yourself," said Echard, "I will shield you and yours; I swear to you that, though I wear this uniform,

and differ from you in creed, your life and
honour shall be as safe as that of my own
sister."

"Oh, sir, what troubles are coming
upon us! this is the day of Gastaldo's
edict. Our home is broken up, our family
is scattered, and from what I saw below
even the very place seems spoiled and
sacked."

"God will support you; we worship
the same God, and I think He will be
more ready to console you under these
trials than to bless us for causing them,
though they are done in the name of
religion."

"Thank you, sir, thank you for pro-
tecting me."

"Thank me not for doing what my
heart prompted, and what will be the
choicest act of my life. May I ask in return that you will remember me; my name
is Echard, and if the day comes when I can
befriend you, I will gladly do so. I came

into this room before I saw you, and spoke kindly to your mother."

"O mother, my darling mother, let me console her; let me tell her there is a generous stranger here, who will protect us. O mother, I feel better; let me rise and comfort her."

Echard was silent; he could not speak, for he was loth to add to the sorrow of one whose beauty and artless manner had already touched his heart. He knew that she was an orphan, but delicacy forbad his interfering with the sacredness of a daughter's woe.

"Mother, dear mother," said Ardoine, approaching the bed and kneeling beside it; "I am here, speak to me. I only left you for a moment; I could not come back sooner; I am here, don't be frightened. Speak to me, dearest mother; it is Ardoine."

She paused: no wonted smile of welcome overspread those pale features; no hallowed blessing bade welcome to the loving child.

Stretching out her hand, she placed it on her mother's forehead; it was cold. The truth flashed upon her; she cast an inquiring look of helplessness at Echard.

" An orphan !—alone !—an orphan !"

The realization was too much; the daughter sank beside the couch, apparently as lifeless as the pale corpse which lay thereon.

CHAPTER XXX.

THE STRUGGLE.

RAYNALD, who had been escorting some of the family to Villar, returned to La Baudène in the evening. As he approached the home of his youth, he was startled by the surrounding marks of desolation and ruin. The meadow was torn up by horses' feet, and the court strewn with fragments of furniture, clothing, books, and household articles, half buried in mud or snow. His thoughts instinctively turned to Ardoine. Had she returned ? Was she safe ? Where was Aunt Marie ? Torn with harrowing fears he rushed to her room, but, in his breathless haste, fell over something that blocked up the stairs leading to that sacred chamber. Raising himself he drew near to the entrance, and held up his hand in the ebbing moonlight. It was wet with blood. In mad frenzy he leaped over the prostrate corpse, and pushed open the shattered door. The fitful light of the moon and the tremulous glare of a torch in the court-yard, enabled him to distinguish objects. His aunt lay in her accustomed place. His senses reeled as he turned and beheld Ardoine lying near her mother, motionless like a corpse, while an officer in uniform was bending over her, and pressing her hand to his lips. A streak of light flitted across the stranger's features, and Raynald recognized him as the bearer of Gastaldo's edict, who had announced this cruel order to the family only three days before, and with whom he had that alterca-tion. Jealousy and indignation fired the heart of Raynald like the flame upon the western prairie. This officer and his soldiers must have glutted their vengeance in the destruction of the farm. He might be the betrayer of Ardoine, as he was the murderer of him who encumbered the stairs. Without doubt it was the corpse of Uncle Jean, who had been left in charge of Aunt Marie and the children.

A sword dripping with blood, whose jewelled handle glittered as the light fell upon it, lay upon the floor. He remembered having seen it in the officer's hand, and it gave cruel confirmation to the dreadful suspicions.

"Wretch!" cried Raynald, rushing upon Echard, "do I meet you again in this once blessed home, as a destroyer and bandit? Have you shed the blood which stains this sword, you who are found alone amid this desolation and havoc?"

In the delirium of passion he grasped Echard with the hand of a giant, and threw him on the floor, while his eyes flashed with the transports of rage, which recks not whether life or death trembles in the balance. Echard, though taken unawares, was not altogether powerless. Coiling his legs round those of Raynald, he caused him to fall forwards, and lose his grasp. Their hands seek each other's throats, they struggle, they writhe, they strain with all the energy of passion and warm-blooded youth.

Raynald is uppermost; he plants his knee upon Echard's breast, and passing his hand across his own forehead to throw back his hair, and recover his senses and sight, gropes for the sword, which he had observed on the floor; grasping it, he brandishes it in the air, before plunging it into his adversary's breast.

" Young man," gasped Echard, " murder not the guiltless, nor outrage the dead. Look at that pale corpse; it has not suffered violence."

The noise of the struggle had meanwhile

aroused Ardoine to consciousness, and with woman's intuition, she comprehended the complex and dangerous misapprehensions. The sword was still in Raynald's hand, and the gripe with which he held Echard was stern and avenging.

" Oh, Raynald, Raynald," cried Ardoine, " stay; he is not the man; he saved me! he saved me! He spoke kindly; I had— I had perished but for him. It was the soldier of the river—Dagot you called him;" and the agonized girl, springing from the bed, under the imparted strength of fear, flung herself between the combatants.

"Oh, Raynald, Raynald—my mother, my mother! She is gone at last. She was alone, and none of us with her to close her eyes. My mother dead—dead!"

"O Lord of heaven," exclaimed Raynald, " are these dreams? are we exiles? Does murder stain this threshold? Has death at this awful time invaded this room? Aunt Marie—art thou gone?—Oh, it is too much—I am bewildered.—Pardon me, sir, if you are guiltless, and are our friend. If you have rescued this sister, you have earned my gratitude, and saved me from another woe. Your heart must plead for the frenzy of sudden and crushing grief."

"Raynald," said Echard, disengaging himself and rising, "Raynald, for such I hear is your name, I can pardon the ravings of a broken heart. I appear to you as a Papal foe, as one who has abetted the havoc and ruin which you see around, but I rejoice to say that I have saved your sister; and I was ready to risk my life to preserve the sanctity of the sick room. Yon corpse at the foot of the stairs is proof of my words. He is one of our soldiers, whose blood you see on my sword. Let that witness that I have been your friend."

"Forgive me," said the young peasant, extending his hand, "forgive me if I have acted hastily. Appearances were against you, and you see enough around to fire any man's blood, especially when I thought that both were corpses."

"Thank God," said Ardoine, "that further bloodshed has been spared, but it is miserable to weep over my lost mother. I thank you again, generous sir, I thank you, and should these troublous times bring any of us into danger, oh befriend us, I beseech you, if it lies in your power."

"I will, I will, I solemnly swear it! Farewell, young mistress! farewell, Raynald!"

Echard's feelings made him loth to leave. He could have lingered anywhere if Ardoine's shadow might but cross his path; but duty summoned him elsewhere. He left the house with a sigh, as he went to search for his horse. From time to time he unconsciously turned his head, peering into the darkness under the vain hope that he might catch another glimpse of her he began passionately to love.

Though he felt the mockery of the

thought, it was like a spell upon his heart—
for the wish was father to the thought.
Driving his spurs into his horse's side, he
plunged into the gathering darkness, and
rode off after his soldiers in the direction
of La Tour.

CHAPTER XXXI.

" Oh, mother," cried Ardoine, after Echard had left, " how can I forgive myself? Alas, was I away when your last summons came? Mother, are you gone, gone for ever?"

" Dearest Ardoine," said Raynald, " do not give way to your feelings. It will make you ill, and you will need your strength and nerve for what may lie before us."

" Oh, Raynald, what shall we do? we are here alone; more soldiers may come; I feel distracted."

" I think the best thing is for me to escort you to Villar, where Father Janavel and most of our family are. I expected some of them back again, but they must have been longer than they anticipated; and now that the darkness has come on with the rain and snow, I should doubt their returning. I know father will; his kind brave heart will bring him back to protect Aunt Marie, and keep Uncle Jean and the children company. But, on the other hand, we cannot tell what misfortunes may have happened to them likewise. But where are Uncle Jean and the children? Have they gone? I see nothing of them."

"Oh, mother, I cannot leave you," cried Ardoine, whose grief made her for a moment heedless of her cousin. "Will you not speak any more? Are you gone at last? Dead—dead. My heart is broken."

"Ardoine, dear Ardoine, you will not derive any benefit from staying here, but, on the contrary, you will expose yourself . to danger. I feel that it is painful for you to leave, but if you will follow my guidance, we will join the rest of our friends. I will place you in safety, and then return and pay honour to the dead. You are not afraid to trust yourself alone to my escort, are you?"

"Raynald," replied Ardoine, weeping bitterly, "how can you ask such a question? Can I be safer than under the protection of one who is dear to me as my own brother?"

"Alas, only as a brother," murmured the young man, as he arranged the room, and waited whilst Ardoine fastened her hood.

"Mother, do I thus leave you? Oh think me not selfish nor unkind! Your soul, I know, is in heaven, with the Saviour whom you loved so much. Alas, this will be the last time that I shall see you, the last time I shall look at that dear face, which I have watched and loved all my life long;" and the bereaved daughter threw herself on the bed, and covered the cold face with burning tears and kisses.

On descending the stairs Raynald was startled at hearing a groan.

"Water, water," cried a feeble voice.

It proceeded from the unfortunate Dagot, in whom life still lingered. Following his generous promptings, Raynald lifted up the wounded man, and carried him across the courtyard into a lower room, where he tried to stanch his wound, while Ardoine ran to the fountain to fetch some water to moisten his lips. The sword had pierced his breast, and as he had fallen backwards the blood had trickled down, and clotted his matted hair. After receiving the water, he uttered a convulsive groan, and relapsed into his previous insensibility. The two cousins then left the farm, and took the road that led to Villar, intending to make a circuit to avoid La Tour, which was filled with soldiers. They had not proceeded far before they heard voices in the distance.

"By Pope Hadrian IV., the English

beggar of St. Albans," said a gruff voice, "this 28th of January is a night to be remembered in these valleys. This edict is a noble work of faith, and will effect a good clearance. What were you telling me, Placido, about that farm that lies on the way where I was this morning?"

"I hear it has been sacked by some of our soldiers," replied Placido Corso, a Romish priest who accompanied the Abbot, "and I fear they have ill-treated its inmates. I heard a report that one of them, who was thinking more of Venus than Mars, has got into trouble."

"Ah," replied Malvicino, "I'll bet the knuckle of St. Anthony he's been after the girl that I saw there, who, I dare say, turned up directly I left."

"What is her name? It begins with an A. By Pope ———, what's become of my memory; it's getting worse. The more's the want of a young housekeeper to keep my accounts. Ardoine, that's her name; I knew it began with an A. I must try and keep her out of old Simond's way, or he and I may clash when we chant our · *Nunc dimittis* next time."

"Simond," said the Abbot aloud, addressing another of his companions, "you're late ; the army has been before the church, and you'll not find much left at this farm, I fear, for your fire brigade. However, let me strip it, if there's anything worth having, before you smash and burn everything, as you did in that Vaudois temple the other day."

"Down with the *barbets*," said Simond, brandishing his large gilt crucifix. "Why, wasn't it with some of this cursed nest that I had the argument one day at La Tour? Argue with them! pull them up root and branch, knock them down with your crucifix; that's what, if I recollect my classics, Aristotle might call an *argumentum ad hominem*."

"We're rather late," soliloquised the

Abbot. "It must be eight o'clock; the Church's work is penitential this cold and dark night; the Abbot must not forget himself."

"I'll warrant," replied Simond, "we'll soon kindle some more light, and be able to read vespers out of our missals by the aid of the bonfire these heretics shall give us. Would," added he, "that we had their bodies on the gridiron, and not the refuse of their goods, which our military apostles have left behind."

"Spirits in purgatory!" said Placido Corso, as he entered the farm, "what have we here? Father Malvicino, here's a wounded soldier; the man's dying—he's dying! Quick, we must absolve him, or it will be too late."

"You can do so," replied Malvicino, "if you are charitably disposed; for myself, I'm too poor to work for nothing. Peter keeps the fees he gets at the gate; I don't transact business for the next world, save on present commission. Confound the girl!" added he aside; "I fear I've lost her."

" Filthy lucre, worthy Abbot, should not keep you from benefiting a man's soul; if his hours in the flames of purgatory can be shortened by your prayers, charity bids you not be silent. Besides, he'll have something; you can take his sword and helmet; he got his wound in fighting here- tics, and a plenary absolution is promised by the Pope to all who assist in this holy work; so I think we must open the door for him, and not keep him outside among the *barbets;* we can shorten his time any- how."

" Give me," said Malvicino, "give me what he's got, we shall get something for them at the Monte di Pieta."

" Poor fellow," said Placido Corso, "his life's ebbing; I'll do what I can for him, as I would for one of these heretics; I would rather convert them by love than by fire and sword, but De La Mèna thinks that the uprooting heretics is agreeable to Moses and well pleasing to God."

Malvicino taking his crucifix from his girdle, held it up before the glazing eye of the dying man.

" *Gnaffe !*" exclaimed he suddenly, as he saw the man's countenance, " By Pope Gregory VII. who—it's the man I sent to catch the girl. There's foul play here; some *barbet* has run him through in the discharge of his duty, and perhaps rescued the girl. I must absolve him, and send him into heaven at once."

Taking two pieces of wood and tying them in the form of a cross, he placed it in Dagot's hand, and hung a small image of the Virgin round his neck. Drawing from his pocket three wax tapers and lighting them, he placed two of them on either side of Dagot's head, and the third in his right hand. The dying man was unable to hold it upright. The scalding wax dropped upon him as he lay upon his back, and the taper, slipping from his grasp, was soon extinguished on the floor.

The Abbot, without loss of time, fell upon his knees and began chanting the Litany for the dying. He dipped a feather into a small phial of oil, and making the sign of the cross on Dagot's forehead, said ;—

"Holy Mary, holy Abel, holy Abraham, all ye holy martyrs, St. Sylvester, St. Gregory, St. Augustine, St. Benedict, St. Francis, pray for him."

"There, Father Placido," said Malvicino, "I think we have shriven him, and may now attend to the wants of the flesh. I'm afraid our sons will have forgotten their spiritual fathers, and have left them nothing to drink."

The dying man groaned heavily; beckoning with his hand to Malvicino to approach, he turned his gory face towards him, and with difficulty gasped out, "It

was the man you call Echard—he—he—
ran—me—through;—the girl—I had
caught her—revenge—me." A ghastly
glare shot through his eye, and the wild
look became fixed. It was stamped in
death.

"Ye popes and anti-popes!" said the
monk aside, "he's spoken to some purpose; the time may come when this knowledge may prove useful, for I have a
grudge against that half-hearted fellow;
he seems much changed since he's been to
Rome. Though I was confessor to the
late Marchioness, he's been very slow in
coming to confess, as if he suspected my
intrigues. I must be careful though, for
he stands well with the Marquis, and has
responsible posts given him. But this may
get him into trouble. I may as well be off
now, and leave my brother to finish the
work. Oh! vengeance to him if he has
supplanted me, and carried off the heretic
Delilah!"

CHAPTER XXXII.

LA BAUDÈNE.

SIMOND was followed by several monks from the convent of La Tour, who arrived at the farm bearing the implements of destruction to finish the work which the military had begun. He placed himself at the head of the ecclesiastics, whose excited passions little needed the incentive of his own fanaticism. Some broke down the doors with pickaxes and crowbars, others threw the contents of the rooms into the central court. The pile increased. Tables, chairs, beds, articles of clothing, books, were hurled into the general chaos. Tearing the leaves out of the Bibles, the monks inserted them into the crevices to quicken the conflagration. The very floors were torn up, and added to the wreck.

"Now then," said Simond, "give me a light."

"Take care, man, the rain will quench it."

"Then I'll fire this *barbet's* manuscript. I'll make a bonfire that shall warm those that are shivering up there on Angrogna's hills."

"There, look out, Irishman," cried Villalmin, addressing O'Donoghue, whose native instincts had brought him back to the scene of wreck and plunder, "or this chair will hit you on the head. There, set it on the top. It's dry wood, and will burn like tinder."

It was Rodolphe's chair. Age and piety could invest it with no charms in the eyes of these outlaws. The cot in which the two little ones had slept the night before was crackling in the blaze, and the

toys of Etienne, Susanne, and Aline were
fuel to the devouring flame. The vines
were uprooted, and the trees of the avenue
felled and cast into the pile.

The rolling flames from this furnace in
the yard now towered aloft, lighting up the
naked outline of the walls, and forming, with
their intervening masses of black smoke,
a gloomy contrast to the snow-clad hills
which the moon revealed beyond. The
monks, with fiendish exultation, danced
round the pile, singing in one chorus—

" Cantet nunc Io,
Chorus Angelorum
Cantet nunc aula cœlestium,
Gloria
in excelsis Deo."

The fire was lighted in those parts of
the building which happened to be standing
or had escaped gutting. The children,
consisting of Susanne, Claude, and Revel,
who had hidden themselves away among

the firewood and casks, had remained there some time half dead with fear, and trusting that Uncle Janavel or Jean might come to their rescue. But they began to feel in their hiding-place the approach of the flames, and were driven from the place of their retreat.

"Father Simond," exclaimed Cattalin, as he saw them in the distance and heard their screams, "here are some of the young vipers. The Holy Office would condemn them to the flames; here you must turn inquisitor; the stake is all ready."

"Come here, my children," said Cattalin, calling out to them; "come, and we will save you from the flames."

Revel hesitated. He stood with his flushed face and black hair conspicuous under the arching flames which showered down the flaking sparks upon him; and looked upon the charred masses which seemed to have intercepted his path.

"Come, sister," said he, taking hold of

Susanne's hand; "I don't understand what is happening. Father and mother are gone; the house seems broken and on fire, and it's so very hot here. Oh can I not pray?" said the child; "God sees me. 'Our Father, which art in heaven, hallowed be Thy name.' Come, sissy, can you say that prayer which Ardoine taught you? There, stand near me. See! that wood is burning and going to drop! Take care—it just missed us! There now, don't scream so, clasp your hands as Ardoine taught you: perhaps we can't get out, and are going to die."

"Oh Ardy, cossy Ardy, where are you?" said the child weeping, and heedless of her brother's words.

"Come, sister, pray as you do every night before you go to bed. Say, 'Our Father.'"

"'Our Father,'" whispered the child.

The gathering flames now drove them more forward, and Cattalin, seeing them, cried—

"So you have crept forth, you heretical cubs. I'll break your bones if you don't cross yourselves and say '*Ave Maria.*'"

"'Our Father, which art in heaven,'" said the two children together in the music of childhood, more sweet amid the roaring crash of their burning home.

"Do you hear?" said the ruffian, raising his sword over Revel's head. "Quick, or I'll cut you. One—two—three—"

"Our Father," replied the child.

The sword descended. The boy fell backward on the ground, and his gashed face was turned upwards. The white froth mingled with the dark blood encrusted his lips, but the spirit had taken its place before the God he had lately addressed as his Father, who was in heaven.

"Come here," said Simond, catching hold of Claude. "Here, Cattalin, help me to hold the wriggling eel. Now, say '*Ave Maria.*'—He won't? Eh? There, give him a dig with your dagger.—Say it; do you hear?

He won't; then give him a prod. Here, lend it me; I'll give him one each time he won't say it," said the minister of religion, in a paroxysm of rage. "Ah! the little beast is dead now."

Susanne had little time to mourn her brother, for the ruffian monk, regardless of the sanctity of childhood, seized her with both his hands, and, bringing her into the court-yard, flung her with all his might on to the funeral pile. The little girl is hurled aloft; her head strikes against fragments of her mother's bed—her garments are in a blaze. The little voice screams, "Oh, Ardy, Ardy, what is this? Ardy, where are you?" and, as if the last impression recurred in the spasms of death, repeats the last words of her brother.

The power of God was seen in perfecting praise in the lips of babes; for He who, in His greatness, condescends to accept the homage of archangels, in His greatness accepts likewise the praises of infant lips.

The fire raged in the court; every now and then a heavy crash was heard, indicating that some wall or chamber was added to the wreck.

"How it burns!" cried Simond; "heap on, heap on! Thus saith the Lord, fire and the sword for the worshippers of Jezebel. These flames are but the shadow of those eternal ones that are being heated seven times in the furnace for heretics. Ah, I only wish we had more of the brood themselves on the top. This is what the Council of Turin should arrange, ' *Congregatio de Propagandâ Fide, et extirpandis Hæreticis.*' "

"Oh, misther clargy, what are you after?" cried O'Donoghue, addressing the ecclesiastic. "Shure and what wark are you making. Was it not enough to turn out the varmin without destroyin' their houses? This was the place that was to be given to some of us Irish, and I had set my heart on it. Arrah, masthers! frinds! Phelim, Tracy, Patrick! ye earned yer wages in killin' these heretics, but they're now robbin' us of our purvision for life."

"Stand out of the way, you mongrel foreigner," said Simond, brandishing a piece of burning wood. "Here, let me get inside to cast a light among that wood-work. Fire the place; how it blazes! Look at it, you dogs of Luther. If I could only get hold of two or three *barbets*, I'd throw ——."

The avenger was near. A large, half-charred beam snapped in two out of the tottering roof, under which Simond was standing, and, striking him on the head, laid him senseless. The unfortunate victim was not seen by his companions, whom the rage of the fire had compelled to retreat. He had fallen not far from the corpse of Dagot. Gradually the fire approaches; the heat recals his senses; he hears the roar—he sees the smoke: he feels the approaching flame—he is unable to move; he groans and curses in the midst of the place, where Rodolphe's voice once faltered in the accents of prayer. Nature was the avenger of the sisters, or rather the evil passions of their persecutors themselves. The fire creeps on; Simond's hair is singed. The flame advances; it recks not whether it be human flesh or wood. There is a taint on the atmosphere as of burning flesh.

*　　*　　*　　*　　*　　*

The flame has rolled on; that fallen monk is visible no more. But should the ashes of that farm be sifted, among the relics would have been found beside the half-melted gilt crucifix calcined bones, and fragments of skulls, the awful testimony that two human beings had perished in the conflagration of the farm of La Baudène.

CHAPTER XXXIII.

MIDNIGHT.

SILENCE once more. The melancholy night of the 28th rolls on, and the snow and rain hiss as they fall upon the lurid embers which smoulder inside the outer walls of La Baudène.

This home, in which the band of sisters dwelt in wedded harmony, presents a mournful contrast to what it was at the opening of the year. A change has come. No waiting wife will stand on that threshold to welcome her husband returning from the labour of the day, or will dance her child in her arms to catch the first glimpse of the coming father; no

husband will again count his homeward
steps until he sees his loving wife expecting his return; no yearning mother will
again marshal her little ones to receive
their grandfather's blessing; no blithe band
of joyous children will frolic over that green
sward, or sport with the gushing fountain;
no snatches of song from the young mountaineer will announce his step over the
quaking pine bridge; no daughter will read
the old man his evening chapter, or soothe
his age, and minister to his wants; no
mothers will again yearn over their sleeping babes; no sufferer will again call forth
the loving tribute of a patriarchal household. Desolation has come. Rome has
offered up this burnt offering to a God of
love, madly dreaming that the God of peace
will accept this impious desecration of
family ties as moral homage to Himself.
They think that He is such a one as themselves; but He will reprove them, and set
before them the things which they have

done. It were to brand heaven itself with infamy to say that it must be peopled by the sword, or that eternal bliss is to be secured by the mutilation of the body, or the desolation of the hearth.

But enough. The Vatican has its triumph; and the ashes of that charred and blasted home are the trophies of that pitiless Church which reigns by thunder and bloodshed, and leagues together the armies and felons of Europe as the apostles of its disfigured creed.

*　　*　　*　　*　　*　　*

Raynald was right in his estimate of his father's character. Considerate of others, and fearless for himself, Janavel had remembered the precarious position of Marie and her band of orphans. Several of the family hoped to have returned early in the afternoon, after depositing their grandfather within the prescribed limits; but difficulty after difficulty had rendered

it impossible. Janavel, however, resolved
to return. His sorrow for the desolation
of his father's home passed into horror
as he approached the place. Before him
gleamed a lurid light, which tinged the outline of the black overhanging clouds, while
fitful shoots of sparks indicated the progress of the flames. The scene which
burst upon him was enough to paralyse his
senses—the buildings inside were a dismantled wreck, the charred, half-consumed
rafter stood out against the dark sky, the
yard was blocked with the scorched *débris*
of the house, the glowing embers of which
were every now and then fanned into a flame
by gusts of wind.

Janavel's thoughts were anxiously turned
to Marie, and he hastened to her apartment, greatly fearing lest she had perished
in the flames. The out-building was, however, standing, and he hoped that she might
have been overlooked amid the general
riot. But when his eye fell upon her,

he saw that she was a corpse. His lion-hearted, yet child-like spirit felt this second shock, for having missed Raynald and Ardoine on the road, he was unprepared for these revelations of pillage and death.

She was alone. She lay, as before, in unruffled calmness, unscathed by the flame. It seemed as if the very fire had respected that saintly relic, and the memories of that dim chamber. She lay in the midst of the devouring flames of crashing timbers and glowing embers, the type of peace upon a battle-field, of hope upon a bed of death.

Janavel fell upon his knees, and gazed fixedly at the corpse. No murmur escaped his lips. He was riveted to the spot. His grief, like that of Job, was too intense for the outlets of common wailing. How time passed he recked not. The distant bell of the convent rang out the midnight hour, and summoned its inmates to *noc-*

turnes. He heard steps approach him ; he heeded not whether it were friend or foe. It is his son. Raynald having conducted Ardoine to a place of safety, and finding his father absent, concluded that he had returned to the farm. Janavel spoke not to his son, and Raynald involuntarily knelt by his side to supplicate Divine support in the hour of trial.

After some time Janavel beckoned to Raynald, and leaving in silence they went into the garden to a large old cypress tree, still standing amid the general wreck. Underneath its dark shadow they began digging. Their mournful labour proceeds without exchange of words. They return to Marie's chamber, and Janavel places his hand on that cold brow, which he now beholds for the last time. Carefully shrouding the body in the coverlid, he carries it down. Overcome by his feelings, he pauses on those stairs still wet with blood, and rests his burden. It is one-and-twenty years since Marie was carried to that chamber, apparently stricken unto death, and she had never since descended. She is borne at last by the feet of them who carry her to the grave.

CHAPTER XXXIV.

THE BURIAL.

MARGUERITE and Renée, who had heard of Raynald's and Janavel's departure, returned that same evening to La Baudène, under the escort of David, accompanied by two or three of the children.

"Oh, Marguerite!" cried Renée, hastening to their sister's room from the outer approach, "where is Marie? Look, her bed is empty! Has some one carried her off? Merciful Father, our griefs are coming in upon us like a flood!"

"Hush, sister; do not give way to grief; you know that Janavel and Raynald were bringing a litter to remove her.

Something unforeseen has, doubtless, hastened their plans. Should this be so, the sooner we return the better, for we can do no good here, and may only expose ourselves to danger."

Little Michel, who was with his mother, could not understand what had happened. He crept upon the foot of the bed, and looked for his aunt.

"Aunty, aunty, where are you?" cried the child; "I have not seen you away before. Mother! has aunty got well, or has she at last gone to heaven? I shall be sorry to miss her, for I have seen her here all my life."

"Marguerite," cried Madeleine, "what is this? The stairs are wet; the yard seems full of broken things, and the main dwelling has no roof, and looks as if it had been burnt. Oh, sister! this is a scene to make us mourners for the rest of our lives."

"Aunt Marguerite," said Etienne, who met her at the door, "I thought I saw somebody like Uncle Janavel and Raynald in the garden, near the old cypress tree; I saw them moving something white, and then I did not see it any more, as if they put it into the ground."

The sisters, joined by some other members of the family who had arrived, went down to the spot. The scene needed no explanation. Janavel and Raynald knelt by the side of a grave. A form lay in that narrow cell. It was Marie! The sisters, the brothers, and the little ones fell on their knees on the cold ground, and in silence wept before God. They were exiles in the heritage of their fathers; their home was a mass of ruins. Even Nature looked friendless. Janavel turned his eye up the valley of Lucerna, and amidst a rent in the clouds the moon shone gloomily on the crags of Castelluzzo.

The tears of the sisters fell into the grave. The one they had cherished lay there, a prey to the ruthless storm. Those lips, so elo-

quent of Christ and his salvation, are sealed
for ever, and the martyred body is com-
mitted stealthily to the ground, for fear of
insults to the dead.   The scenes of past
joy floated before the minds of the mourners, who felt the sad presage of a disastrous
future.   But mark! there is sympathy in
nature for human grief.   The rude blast
which moaned at intervals, and swept over
the face of the dead, has become hushed;
and a bright symbol of purity and beauty
is sent them from heaven.

The snow falls into the grave.   Marie
is being gradually entombed.   The outlines
of a form, under the covering of snow, in-
dicates that there reposes a human body.
It is unscathed—a contrast to the two
bodies which the fire entombed.   The
snow-flakes fall fast; the eyes of all are
bent on the grave, when the solemn voice
of Janavel is heard repeating—

"'Though your sins be as scarlet, they
shall be as white as snow:' our beloved

sister had washed her robes and made them white in the blood of the Lamb, before whom her spirit now stands with joy unspeakable and full of glory."

White as the light floating from heaven, like the down of an angel's wing—softly, silently did the snow fall, until it covered the dead. It was a winding-sheet which neither art nor affection could supply, but God alone. Marie can be seen no more. She is buried! It was Nature's lamentation, and Nature's funeral, like herself, sublime, yet beautiful—simple, yet grand.

END OF VOL. I.

APPENDIX.

CHAPTER I.

Extract from the Bull of Pope Innocent VIII. for the Extirpation of the Waldenses, A.D. 1487.

THE original is in Volume G of the Cambridge Manuscripts, and the translation is from Sir Samuel Morland's History, page 197, to which reference may be made at the British Museum :—

"We have heard, and it is come to our knowledg, not without much displeasure, that certain sons of iniquity, inhabitants of the province of Evreux, followers of that abominable and pernicious sect of malignant men who are called the poor people of Lyons, or the Waldenses, who have long ago endeavoured in Piemont and other neighbouring parts, by the procurement of him who is the sower of evil works, through by-ways purposely sought out, and hidden precipices, to insnare the sheep belonging unto God, and at last to bring them to the perdition of their souls by deadly cunning, are damnably risen up under a feigned pretence of holiness, being led into a reprobate sense, and do greatly erre from the

way of truth; and following superstitious and heretical ceremonies do say, act, and commit very many
things contrary to the orthodox faith, offensive to the
eyes of the Divine majesty, and which do occasion a
very great hazard of souls."

Pope Innocent X. was guilty of an intrigue with
his brother's widow, Donna Olympia Maldachini.

The most remarkable transaction of this Pontifi-
cate was his Bull, 31st May, 1653, condemning the
five propositions selected by the Jesuits out of Jansenius's Augustinus, which ultimately gave rise to
the famous question whether the infallibility of the
Pope extended to matters of fact, or only to matters
of doctrine.

CHAPTER II.

EXTRAORDINARY as it appears, this chapter is based
on fact; the extracts from Léger and Dr. Muston
are given in the Preface. The truthfulness of this
fact is the best apology for its singularity, and must
vindicate the author from the charge of making an
improbable hypothesis the basis of his story.

CHAPTER IV.

THE character of Marie is sketched from life. The
original was a poor person whom I was in the habit
of visiting when at college. She was confined to her
bed for twenty-seven years without once leaving her
room; nearly all the speeches in Marie's mouth are
real experiences of suffering uttered by this person,
as, owing to her blindness I was able to take down
her words in pencil at the time of their utterance.

This circumstance, as it clothes them with the moral value of true experiences of Christian suffering, will explain their peculiar style.

CHAPTER VI.

THE destruction of the Vaudois temples was of frequent occurrence during their great, or desultory persecutions. The abbey of Pignerol used to retain a body of armed men in its pay, to make incursions into the valleys.—*Muston*, vol. i. p. 277, *Gilles History*.

In the month of May, 1636, the Monk Simound assailed some peaceable Vaudois, whom he found in the market-place of La Torre, with gross abuse; and then, holding a gilt crucifix in his hands, he fell on his knees uttering curses against the reformed kings and princes. Evidently he hoped to irritate the by-standers, both by his crucifix, before which he knelt, and by his unseemly language.—*Monastier's History of the Vaudois Church*, p. 249.

CHAPTER VIII.

THE conversation in this chapter is entirely historical, see *Léger*, part ii., chap. vi., p. 72.

CHAPTER XI.

THIS scene is founded on fact, see *Léger*, part ii., p. 348.

CHAPTER XII.

THE extracts are taken *verbatim* from the Waldensian Catechism, and the concluding incident from *Dr. Muston*, vol. i., p. 262, who gives a copious list of his various authorities.

CHAPTER XIII.

As regards the number of soldiers quartered on the valleys, see *Léger*, part ii., p. 177, 180.

CHAPTER XV.

I HAVE been an eye-witness of a similar scene on the " Scala Santa." The general description is accurate.

As regards the Papal Tariff for the remission of sins, the reader may consult *Histoire des Souverains Pontifes, qui ont siégé a Avignon*, par Joudou, August, 1855. I obtained this book at Avignon in May last, although it had been suppressed by the Romish clergy. The following is an extract, page 125, vol. i., with the foot note. One or two quotations are taken from the *Pièce Justificative*, for the edification of the English sceptic, though many of the taxed crimes are such, " that it is a shame even to speak of them." I met with a similar document and tariff when travelling in Spain a few years ago :—

" Le trésor de la chancellerie avait été pillé par les familiers de Clément V. ; l'escarcelle pontificale était vide, il fallait aviser aux moyens de la remplir. En 1319, Jean XXII., pour remédier à cette pénurie, établit, à son profit, des réserves sur tous les bénéfices des églises collégiales de la Chrétienté ; il vendit des indulgences et l'absolution de tous les crimes ; il ordonna la levée d'une taxe, par laquelle, moyennant

un prix déterminé, les attentats, même les plus hor-
ribles, étaient acquitteés.*

Pièce Justificative, No. 1, page 126. Traduction
de quelques articles de la taxe de la chancellerie
apostolique pour la rémission des péchés.

" Si un ecclesiastique commet le péché de la chair,
soit avec des nonnes, soit avec ses cousines, ses nièces
ou des filleules, soit enfin avec toute autre femme, la
coupable sera absous pour la somme de 67 livres
12 sous.

" Les prêtres qui voudront obtenir l'autorisation de
vivre en concubinage avec leurs parentes paieront
76 livres 1 sou.

" L'absolution du meurtre simple commis sur un
laique est taxée a 15 livres 4 sous 3 deniers ; si
l'assassin a tué plusieurs hommes dans la journée, il
n'en paiera pas davantage.

" Pour le meurtre d'un frère, d'une sœur, d'une
mère ou d'un pére, on paiera 17 livres 15 sous.

" Celui qui voudra acheter par avance l'absolution
de tout meurtre accidentel qu'il pourrait commettre a
l'avenir, paiera 168 livres 15 sous.

" Un hérétique qui se convertit, paiera pour son
absolution 269 livres. Le fils d'un hérétique brûlé
ou mis à mort par tout autre supplice, ne pourra être
réhabilité qu'en payant à la chancellerie 218 livres
16 sous 9 deniers.

" Un ecclésiastique qui ne pourra pas payer ses

---

* Cette constitution de Pape Jean XXII. existe et a eu
plusieurs editions ; elle est intitulée : Taxæ sacræ cancellaria·
apostolicæ, et taxæ sacræ pœnitentiariæ itidem apostolicæ.

dettes et qui voudra éviter les poursuites de ses créanciers donnera au pape 17 livres 8 sous 6 deniers, et sa créance lui sera remise.

" La permission de dresser des boutiques de marchands et de vendre différentes denrées sous le portique d'une église sera accordée moyennant 45 livres 19 sous 3 deniers.

" Pour faire la contrebande et frauder les droits du prince on paiera 87 livres 3 deniers.

" Un moine vertueux qui voudra passer sa vie dans un ermitage ver sera dans le tresor du pape 45 livres 19 sous.

" Si un homme veut acquerir par simonie un ou plusieurs bénéfices, il s'adressera aux trésoriers du pape, qui lui vendront à un prix modéré.

" Celui qui voudra manquer à son serment et être garanti de toute poursuite et de toute infamie, paiera au pape 131 livres 15 sous."

(Comment on the above is superfluous.)

CHAPTER XVII.

THE principal authority for this chapter is *Gilles.*

CHAPTER XVIII.

THE edict is given *verbatim;* the original may be seen in Italian and French in *Léger*, part ii., p. 92. The translation of the portion in the text is from *Sir Samuel Morland*, p. 303.

"Andrew Gastaldo, Doctor of the Civil Law, Master Auditor Ordinary, sitting in the most illustrious Chamber of Accompts of His Royal Highness and Conservator-general of the holy Faith, for the

observation of the Orders, published against the
pretended Reformed religion of the valley of Lucerna
and St. Martino, and upon this account particularly
deputed by His said Royal Highness. We do command and charge the chief sworn messengers of the
Court to give commandment and injunction, even as
by these presents we command and enjoyn every
head of a family with its members of the pretended
Reformed religion, of what rank, degree, or condition
soever (none excepted), inhabiting and possessing
estates in the places of Lucerna, Lucernetta, S. Giovanni, La Torre, etc.

"Within three days after the publication and
execution of these presents, to withdraw and depart,
and to be with their families withdrawn out of the
said places, and transported into the places and
limits tolerated by His Royal Highness, and by his
good pleasure, as, viz., Bobbio, Villaro, Angrogna,
Rorata, and the country of Bonetti under pain of
death and confiscation of houses and goods, situated
or being out of the said limits, *Provided always in
case they do not make it appear to us within twenty days
following that they are become Catholicks, or that they
have sold their goods to the Catholicks.*"

CHAPTER XXIV.

NOT one word of this description is exaggerated,
as may be verified by referring to *Léger*, part ii.,
chap. viii., p. 94, and *Morland*, p. 305. The passage
is most plaintive and interesting, but too long for
quotation; its details are, however, embodied in the
text.

CHAPTER XXV.

FOR an account of the massacre of the Protestants by the Irish in 1641, see Clarendon's *History of the Rebellion*, vol. i., book iv., page 237; and Hume's *History of England*, vol. vi., chap. lv., page 383, the details of which, too horrible to be transcribed, were repeated by the same agents, the Irish, aided by the Piedmontese, in the Italian valley of Lucerna in 1655. As regards the part assigned to the Irish in these transactions, independently of the testimony of Newland and Léger, Hume informs us, vol. vii., chap. lx., page 151—"The Irish were glad to embrace banishment as a refuge. Above forty thousand men passed into foreign service; and Cromwell, well pleased to free the island from enemies who never could be cordially reconciled to the English, gave them full liberty and leisure for their embarkation." See Clarendon's *History of the Rebellion*, vol. iii., book xii., page 278.

CHAPTER XXXII.

As regards the results of Gastaldo's order, and the consequent desolation and pillage, see *Léger*, part ii., p. 96. The incident of Claude's death is founded on the deaths of Jaques Ronc, *Léger*, part ii., p. 126, and *Daniel Rambaut*, p. 135; also see *Morland*, p. 370.

HARRILD, PRINTER, LONDON.

www.ingramcontent.com/pod-product-compliance
Lightning Source LLC
Chambersburg PA
CBHW030949110726
47900CB00004B/1187